Tunnel to Tar-Ra

Susan E Boyer

Tunnel to Tar-Ra
First edition published in Australia, June 2024

Published by Birrong Books,
(Imprint of Boyer Educational Resources)
PO Box 255, Glenbrook, NSW, 2773, Australia
www.birrongbooks.com
boyer@birrongbooks.com

Copyright © Susan E Boyer

ISBN: 9781877074073

A catalogue record for this
book is available from the
National Library of Australia

Cover artwork by Julie McVey, www.juliemcvey.com.au
Cover graphics completed by Matt Thompson.

Typeset in 11/14pt Calibri

Printed by Lightning Source.

Information for Indigenous Australian communities:

Readers, please be aware that this book contains names of deceased persons which in some Indigenous Australian communities may offend cultural prohibitions.

Dedicated to the memory of
Susan E Boyer
1953 – 2022

Tunnel to Tar-Ra

Shoreline of Sydney Cove.
Adaption of a map created in 1822.
Showing places visited by the time slip visitors in 1791.
Source: National Library of Australia - nla.obj-229911701-1

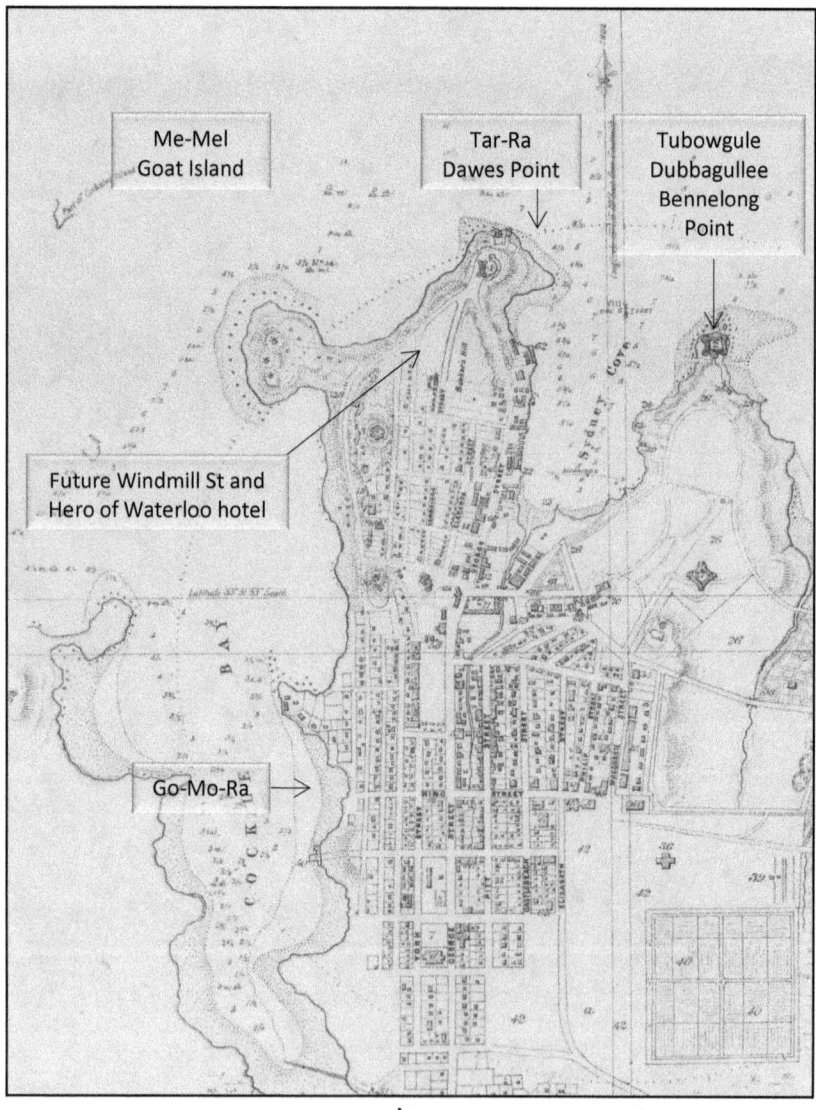

Me-Mel
Goat Island

Tar-Ra
Dawes Point

Tubowgule
Dubbagullee
Bennelong
Point

Future Windmill St and
Hero of Waterloo hotel

Go-Mo-Ra

Tunnel to Tar-Ra

Modern Sydney shoreline – 2020s
Source: Maps Data: Google©2024

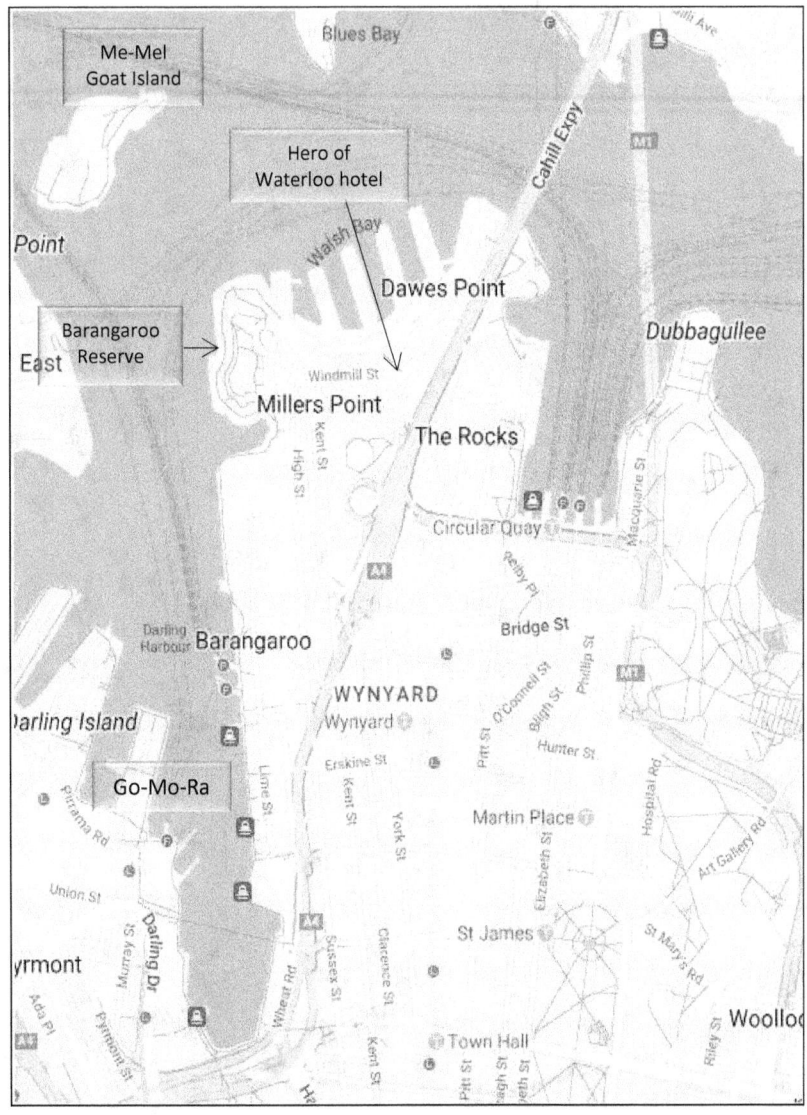

Tunnel to Tar-Ra
A View of Sydney Cove, Port Jackson, Australia, 7th March 1792, by a Port Jackson Painter

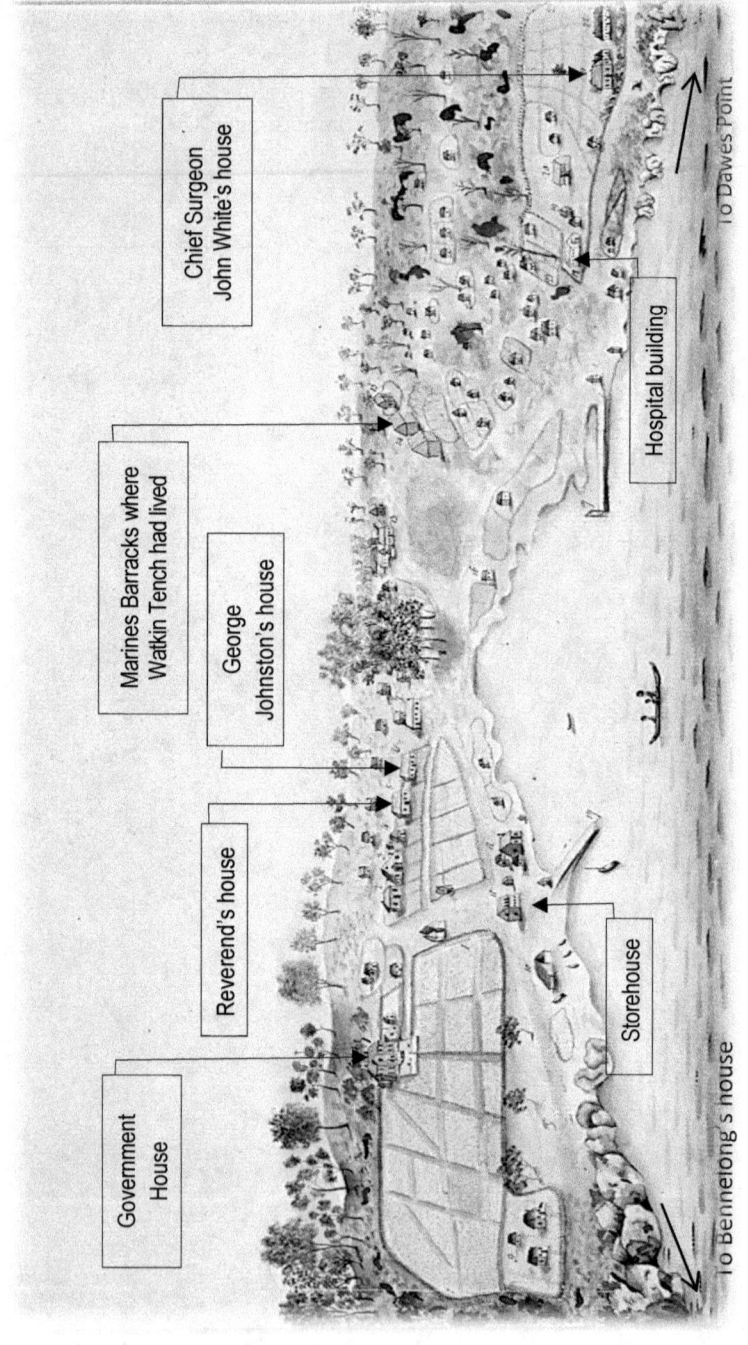

Government House

Reverend's house

Marines Barracks where Watkin Tench had lived

George Johnston's house

Chief Surgeon John White's house

Hospital building

Storehouse

To Dawes Point

To Bennelong's house

Tunnel to Tar-Ra

Contents

Tunnel to Tar-Ra
... and another world
Prologue

Sydney Daily News Online

Sensational find near archaeological site

Archaeologists are mystified by the discovery of a pair of sports shoes found in an archaeological excavation near 'The Big Dig' in The Rocks. This site contains artefacts from the late 18th century, the time of Australia's first European settlement.

The find has been dubbed a hoax by commentators who say the only way such modern items could come to be there is by someone placing them there as a prank. When asked how the pranksters could have achieved such a feat – burying footwear far below the city's current level – they suggested it was done after the site was disturbed, and then carefully covered over to be 'discovered' by inexperienced volunteers working on-site.

This claim was dismissed when scientists revealed the items were located with a geophysical technique known as ground penetrating radar (GPR), a method which provides information about what's in the ground before digging it up. The flaw of GPR is that, while it can detect items, it cannot provide accurate dating.

Some say the discovery could be an example of *Out of Place Artefacts* or *OOPArt*, which are defined as relics of archaeological, historical or paleontological interest found 'out of context'. These finds challenge accepted historical chronology by their presence in unexpected places. Author and leader in the field, J. H. Brennan, suggests such finds could support the possibility of time travel. However, critics of OOPArt say these discoveries are either hoaxes, mistaken interpretation or wishful thinking.

For now, scientists are keeping an open mind until further tests are carried out.

Chapter 1

Windmill Street

The Rocks, Sydney

'Psst!' The sound came from the wall beside the pavement. Archie slowed his step and looked around. For a second, he thought it was guys from school with their heckling, but Windmill Street was almost deserted. He could hear the constant drone of traffic on the Cahill Expressway and sirens wailing from the city beyond, but the only visible sign of life was a couple walking a dog up the hill.

Where's the usual crazy rush?

He continued up the hill trying to quell his uneasiness, but his mouth felt dry and his armpits clammy. Even the sky had an odd, eerie glow. *More bushfires in the mountains?*

'Psst!' The muffled sound came again. 'In here!' a hissy voice added. This time it seemed to come from a low vent in the wall at pavement level.

Archie kept walking.

He knew the narrow opening was a light shaft into the cellar of the Hero of Waterloo hotel – he'd passed it a hundred times. But today the thick cobwebs between the iron bars spooked him. He quickened his pace and was nearly at the corner when he sensed movement behind and then felt a hand on his shoulder.

'What the …!' Archie spun around ready to take a swing.

'It's me, Arch!' Oliver whispered as he beckoned Archie through a stone arch in the wall. Archie found himself in a dark, sandstone-lined storage area.

'Far out, bro! Why the secrecy?' Archie barked as Oliver signalled him to keep quiet, at the same time leading the way along a low stone-flanked passage.

'I thought you weren't allowed down here,' Archie queried,

3

finding himself in the cool cellar beneath the Hero.

'I'm not – but didn't you hear the news this morning?' Oliver cleared his throat and took on the voice and pose of a newsreader: 'Anyone with breathing problems … is advised to stay indoors … due to poor air quality.'

Archie noticed for the first time that Oliver was wheezing; his shorts and t-shirt were covered in dirt and he had smudges on his face and knees.

'Dad said to stay indoors cos of my asthma,' Oliver continued in his own voice. 'It's no big deal; no-one need know we're down here anyway.' He grinned, opening his hand to reveal a clutch of keys.

'Yeah, it's hazy out there,' Archie changed the subject to hide his discomfort. 'I tried calling but …'

'Huh, no reception down here, but I was watching for you heading up the hill, to catch you before you got to the corner. Dad's at a meeting till late, and the staff upstairs – well, no need to bother them.'

The passage opened into a larger space lined with sandstone blocks and large uneven slabs underfoot. Boxes and crates lined one wall but it looked like it had been a tavern room at one time.

An enormous disused fireplace was set into one of the walls and arched alcoves led off the others. Huge, blackened bellows lay next to the hearth and a stone trough stood on a raised platform on the opposite side. An old rocking chair, a metal milk urn, and various cast-iron pots, kettles and tools completed the scene.

'Looks like a museum down here,' Archie said, looking around.

'Yeah, that's Dad's plan one day I s'pose.'

'Hi Arch.' Millie waved from the corner, pulling AirPods from beneath her dark bobbed hair. She sat propped against the wall with a book open on her lap and a packet of corn chips on the floor beside her. 'Convicts used to get chained up over there,' she said, nodding in the direction of heavy chains hanging from metal rings attached to the far wall.

'Geez,' was all Archie got out before Oliver demanded his attention again.

'Wait till you see what I've found over here,' he said, beckoning Archie towards a dimly lit alcove. He pointed to the back of the recess, where part of an earthen floor had been uncovered to reveal wide timber planks. Oliver ducked beneath the stone lintel and stood next to his find.

'Listen!' he announced, stamping on the boards 'it's hollow!'

'Wow!' Archie blurted, prompting Millie to put her book aside and join them.

'What is it?' she asked, squinting towards her brother.

'I tried telling you before Mil, but you wouldn't get your head out of that book. It's a sort of hatchway I think, or maybe a hiding spot for something.' His voice radiated excitement.

'How'd you find it, Ollie?' Archie moved closer and knelt to knock on the boards. It was definitely hollow beneath.

'I was moving things around cos I was bored, and at the back here, under a heap of stuff, the floor felt kinda, you know, echoey. So I scraped the dirt away and found this ... sort of ... trapdoor. I've tried to open it but there's nothing to grip on to ...' He sat back on his haunches and looked at Archie. 'So we might have to try levering the boards ...'

'No, Ollie,' his sister piped up. 'Just leave it, will you!'

'Leave what?' said a fourth voice.

Millie jumped and spun around, and the boys peered warily from the alcove to see Jemima standing near the entrance, clearly amused by their stunned expressions. She hoped their surprise was due to her latest look: a half-shaved head with the remaining black curls streaked vivid red. Her bare scalp revealed a tattooed Southern Cross along the hairline, accentuating a row of brow piercings.

Archie wondered what their mum would say this time. She'd let the tattoo go, and then the piercing, but now the shaved scalp just drew attention to them. His sister looked plain weird. He could hear his mother saying, 'You'll never get a job looking like that!'

'Oh, it's only you, Jem.' Oliver said with a deep exhale. 'How'd you know we were here?'

'When I turned into Windmill Street, I saw Archie disappear through the side entry, so I figured you must all be here. You're not supposed to be down here though, are you?' she said, looking at her cousins, then her brother.

'Well …' Archie began.

'It's cos of the air out there,' Millie cut in, returning to her book corner and corn chips, 'and Ollie's asthma,' she continued, plonking herself back on the floor. She was about to elaborate when Jemima, apparently satisfied with the explanation, came to sit next to her.

'You should've locked the door behind you though,' Jemima called to Oliver as he disappeared into the recess again. 'Don't worry, I've bolted it,' she added, before turning to Millie.

'What do you think?' she said, before quickly adding, 'Not about the hair – about this?' She swivelled her phone screen towards her younger cousin.

'A bit old for you, isn't he?' said Millie, staring at the good-looking face on the screen.

'Not for me! For Mum – it's time she moved on. I've been checking dating sites for her.'

'What does *she* think about that?' Millie asked, intrigued by her cousin's pluck.

'She doesn't know yet, but she needs a push. We're not moving back with Dad,' Jemima said before falling into silence. Millie opened her mouth to say something but changed her mind.

'So, what're you reading, bookworm?' Jemima asked,

flipping Millie's book cover. '*Stories of Life at Sydney Cove*,' she mouthed. 'Oh, yawn! Boring history. Why don't you read something, like, exciting?'

'Knew you'd say that, but it is. It's stories of kids – sent to a convict prison ship in England and what happened when they got *here*.' Seeing the sparkle in her cousin's eye, Jemima didn't have the heart to mock.

'Just picture it through their eyes Jem, looking from the ship to the shore? No buildings, no roads – nothing but wilderness. Knowing they'd be sleeping in tents and thinking there were cannibals lurking outside?'

'Cannibals?'

Millie chuckled, seeing she had Jemima's interest. 'Pretty ignorant, eh?' A sudden creaking of timber cut into their conversation.

'What're you guys up to?' Jemima called.

'Come take a look,' said Oliver, poking his head around the wall. The girls scrambled to their feet and headed over to see him removing timbers to expose a gaping hole in the floor.

'What the …?' Jemima blurted on seeing the cavity and the split planks beside it.

'No big deal, Jem?' Oliver shrugged. 'I can put the timber back, cover it over and no-one has to know.'

Jemima rolled her eyes but said nothing.

'But we should at least have a peek first, don't you think?' Oliver suggested with a grin.

Despite herself, Jemima edged closer. The four of them huddled over the shaft, feeling its cool, earthy upward draught. As their eyes adjusted, worn stone steps became visible, leading into murky blackness.

'Wanna take a proper look down there?' Oliver whispered into the opening.

'No!' the others reacted in unison.

Jemima glared at her cousin, spreading her hands in disbelief. 'What about your asthma?'

But Oliver stared back with a look that said *What wimps!* 'It's easing up.'

'She's right, Ollie,' Archie said, eyes fixed on the yawning hole. 'We should give it a miss.' He had imagined uncovering a shallow hiding place for money or valuables, but there was no way he was lowering himself into that deep cavity. He didn't like dark, closed-in spaces.

'There could be rats, or anything,' Millie added, bolstered by Archie's stance.

'Well, I'm having a look!' Ollie said, flicking on his phone's torch decisively. 'It's been covered so long that anything down there'd be well and truly dead. It's probably just another storeroom.'

'What if there *is* something dead, Ollie?' Archie now had a vision of skeletons around the walls. 'It's not a good idea,' he added, shoving his hands in his pockets.

'Oh, don't be so dramatic, you lot. Shine my torch down there, Archie, while I have a look.'

Seeing he wasn't to be put off, Archie took Oliver's phone and held it up as Oliver lowered himself into the hole and felt his way down the steps. The others watched in silence as his head disappeared below the floor. Archie felt a knot of discomfort at his wimpiness, at the same time sensing a delicious, ghoulish curiosity oozing up his spine.

'Okay,' Oliver's arm reached out of the darkness. 'Hand me the torch, Arch.' Moments later his voice came with an echoey quality, 'Geez, it's pitch black down here – but I can stand up.'

'Be careful, will you!' Millie piped, knowing her brother

wouldn't listen.

'Hang on,' he called, before a long pause.

The others leaned into the cavity, seeing nothing but light beams flicker this way and that.

'Nope, no skulls or skeletons,' he called, followed by a mocking laugh. A second later his voice came in an excited shriek. 'Actually, it seems like the start of a tunnel!'

The other three looked at each other and then back at the hole.

'It is!' he confirmed, sounding more muffled and distant.

'Get back here right now, Ollie!' Millie yelled, surprising herself with her forcefulness.

'Okay, okay ...' Oliver sounded slightly breathless now. There was a shuffle, the light stilled and then there was silence.

'Ollie?' Archie called. 'You okay, mate?' They waited but there was no reply.

****

Chapter 2

The Tunnel

'Oliver!' Millie shouted through the hatch, but still nothing.

Jemima put her hand over her mouth to stifle a groan. It was impossible to see into the hole, as Oliver's phone light was shining upwards. Archie stared wide-eyed into the inkiness.

'I'll have to go down there,' he announced, feeling a sudden surge of adrenaline. He went to push the others aside.

'No, I'm going!' Jemima insisted, propelling herself forwards. 'I'm the eldest,' she said under her breath as she backed into the hole with her eyes closed.

The steps were narrow and steep; her right arm brushed a side wall as she descended. It felt coarse and cold. As the coolness lapped at her cheeks, she opened her eyes and allowed them to adjust. Her heart was thumping. She couldn't see anything except the stone wall flanking the steps to her right. The other side was a black abyss beyond the beam of Oliver's phone. She desperately wanted to shine a light below her but she needed both hands to feel her way.

'Ollie?' she enquired gently. Her voice sounded hollow against the silence. An earthiness tickled her nostrils; the back of her neck tingled.

'Can you see him, Jem?' Archie's voice came shakily from above.

'Not yet,' she called, continuing to feel her way down the steps until her foot touched level ground.

As she took her phone from her pocket and flicked on the torch, she sensed movement to her side, then a muffled sound, like a grunt. She spun around in mute panic, the light arcing across the stone floor to make out a huddled form against the wall. It was Oliver with a hand over his mouth, his eyes blinking wildly against the beam. She struggled to stop her hands trembling, to still the torch. Then, in a flash of relief and fury, she realised he had his hand over his mouth and that he was stifling his own nervous amusement.

'Can you see him?' Millie called through the shaft again.

'Yes,' was all Jemima could manage for a second. 'He's okay,' she added flatly.

'What's happened? Why can't we hear him?' Archie called in a manner that said he was preparing for a bad report.

'He's okay!' Jemima yelled, trying to control her temper.

'We're coming down,' Millie called, but Jemima didn't hear her. With her light still aimed at Oliver's face, she glared at Oliver with a clenched jaw. 'You *are* okay, aren't you? You little – argh!'

He nodded but didn't say a word; his lips were pressed tightly as if to suppress a spurt of laughter. But his body language suggested he knew he'd gone too far. He sat hunched, elbows on knees, cupping his hands to the sides of his face.

Jemima looked away. Her eyes had adjusted sufficiently to take in the enclosed space; it had the dimensions of a spacious elevator and was empty but for the two of them. She realised her anger had overtaken the fear she would usually feel in such a dark confined area.

'So is this your idea of a joke?' She still stood over Ollie, hissing into his face.

'Well – it was just a spur-of-the-moment thing, Jem.'

By now Millie and Archie had reached the bottom of the steps but they still couldn't see Oliver.

'What's going on?' Archie leaned forwards with concern in his voice, not convinced all was well. All he could make out was a dark mass against one of the walls until Jemima shone her phone light onto it. They stood frowning down at Oliver.

'Look, it was just a joke; seemed funny at the time.' Oliver said, scrambling to his feet. 'It's no big deal and it got you all down here, didn't it?'

'Geez mate,' Archie scowled, and kicked the flagstones.

'How could you be so mean, Ollie?' Millie spat the words. 'We thought ...'

'Well, I'm okay. Does *sorry* help?'

'No!' said Millie, folding her arms in a huff.

Archie made no comment.

'But it's true. If I hadn't got the ball rolling, you'd never've stepped through that hatchway. Admit it!' Oliver held his hands wide as if offering them a gift.

'That's not the point and you know it. When will you grow up, Ollie?' Jemima blew out a long sigh. 'Oh, you're impossible,' she added in a lighter tone.

She flicked her light into the corners and across the uneven stone above their heads but there wasn't so much as a spider's web in sight. She felt an unexpected impulse to explore.

'I guess since we *are* here, we may as well check out this tunnel you've found.' She was peering into the shadows, searching for an opening. 'Or, on second thoughts, was that a joke too?' she added, swiftly turning to her cousin.

'No, it's not a joke – look.'

He swung his light into the far corner where a deep recess came into focus. He stepped towards it and Jemima followed. Archie and Millie looked at each other, both hoping the other would protest, but after a brief hesitation, they trailed after them.

If they can do this, so can I, Archie told himself. Now that their eyes had adjusted, it wasn't so daunting. Light was still spilling through the hatchway above. Oliver had his phone light reassuringly lighting the way to show the tunnel was wide enough for them to be two abreast.

A short way in, Jemima cast her light across the sandstone block walls, where she spotted curious markings etched into the stone.

'Is that initials cut into the rock?' she asked, stopping to trace the deep indents.

'Could be,' said Archie. 'Looks like an *H*, and *K* maybe. I wonder how long that's been here?' he said, forcing his tone to sound even.

'Come on,' Oliver called from several paces ahead. 'I wanna see what's down there.'

'Not much further, Ol,' Jemima said in a decisive manner.

They continued along the passage following Oliver's light, and with each step they began an imperceptible descent.

'I bet this was for smuggling in the old days.' Oliver's voice was infused with anticipation.

'It's spooky,' Millie whispered, '... but fun.' She was pleased and impressed by her bravery.

'We're only going a bit further, guys,' Jemima piped from the rear.

'Nah, it'll come to a dead end soon,' Oliver assured them before embarking on a story of drunken men kidnapped and taken to ships on the waterfront. 'They probably used secret tunnels like this!' he said, contradicting his dead-end theory.

Jemima nudged Millie and rolled her eyes. But Millie was only half listening to Oliver's ramble. The initials etched into the walls had her thinking about the chains hanging in the cellar. Vague images hovered at the edge of her mind, but evaporated into the darkness as her brother's voice cut into her thoughts.

'You know what *shanghaied* means, don't you?' Oliver called over his shoulder. 'It's when a guy was too drunk to know what's what and they'd take him to the ship – through passageways like this.'

Jemima snorted loudly but Oliver ignored her, continuing his story as he led the way with confident strides, still holding up his phone to light their way.

'It's true. When they sobered up they were already on the high seas, no sight of dry land – no way of escape.' When Jemima let out another mocking laugh, he spun around, casting darting lights around the passage. 'We saw it in a movie, didn't we Arch?'

'Anyway,' Jemima interrupted. 'This was meant to be a *quick* look. It seems to keep going Ollie so let's head back ...'

Oliver kept walking as if he hadn't heard.

'And,' Millie added, looking over her shoulder. 'I can't see light from the shaft anymore. It's too creepy now.'

Hearing that, Archie turned to gauge how far it was back to the steps. Seeing the walls behind him merge into blackness, his heart began thumping. He gulped at the air to calm himself. 'Yeah,' he agreed. 'Come on, let's go, Ollie.'

'Look, it's getting narrower now, which proves we're near a dead end,' Oliver announced, still walking. 'We have to see what's there.'

'That wasn't the deal,' Millie yelled at her brother. 'I don't like this; I can't breathe! I want to go back!'

'Me too, but my phone only has one per cent battery left; it's going to die any sec,' Jemima said, squinting at the screen. 'Where's yours?' she said, looking from Millie to Archie.

'I left it in my backpack. I didn't think ...' said Archie.

Millie's expression said likewise.

'Okay, we'll make Ollie go back. Come on,' Jemima said, quickening her pace to catch up with him. 'Stop now, Ollie!' she roared with a harshness that echoed through the darkness.

When she caught up with him, Oliver turned quickly and shone the light in her face. 'Geez, you look spooky, Jem, with that hair,' he said with a chortle.

'Ollie!' she repeated, angry enough to hit him. 'We're going back. We need your phone. Mine's almost dead,' she said, holding out her hand. 'Hand it over, Ollie,' she repeated, cutting off his protest. 'We're going back!' She went to snatch the phone but Oliver pulled away.

'Look, we can't turn back now, cuz ...'

'Oh yes, we can, and we are!'

'Okay, okay, you win, but just wait *one* sec while I check down there.'

Jemima and Millie glared at him. Archie opened his mouth to object.

'I don't *care* what's there! My phone's dead. I have no light,' Jemima said through gritted teeth.

'Okay, take it,' he said, holding his phone out to her. But as she snatched it from Oliver's hand, shards of light darted around the cavity, blinding her. Amid loud curses, the phone teetered midair, before falling with a clatter onto the stone flagging. Instantly it was so dark Jemima couldn't see her hand in front of her face. They were swathed in a blackness so dense it felt like a weight against their skin.

****

Chapter 3

Disorientation

No-one spoke for several seconds. In the complete absence of light, the air felt thick and heavy, its earthiness intensified. Archie felt the darkness seep between his collar and the back of his neck. He felt his gut clamping, his throat choking, as the blackness pressed against him. He couldn't speak.

'You idiot!' Jemima blurted into the silence. 'Look what you've done, Ollie! It'd better not be broken.'

'Don't blame me! It wasn't my fault. You should've grabbed it.'

'It doesn't matter whose fault it is,' Millie cut in. 'Let's just find the phone. Jem, don't you have *any* light left?'

'Nope,' Jem replied sullenly, dropping to her haunches and feeling around her feet. The others did the same, sliding their backs down the wall. No-one spoke while they pawed the ground in broadening circles, the darkness amplifying their shallow breathing.

'How come it's *so* dark? I mean ...' Archie tried to keep his voice level but couldn't disguise a tremor.

'Let's just find the phone, Arch. It must've bounced or slid away. We need to check further out.'

In the process of crawling and fumbling in the darkness they repeatedly bumped into each other. They felt each other's anxiety through the blackness as their huffs and grunts echoed off the walls.

'Get your butt out of my way,' Jemima snarled at no-one in particular. 'Why did we listen to your stupid idea, Oliver?' She spat the words, her voice sounding out of control. By this stage their frantic search had come to an exhausted stall.

'Actually, it was *your* idea, remember,' Oliver mumbled.

'This is ridiculous,' Archie said, sinking against the wall. 'The stupid thing *has* to be here. It can't just vanish! Come on, spread out more. It could've slid out in any direction.'

After more rummaging and heated words, their efforts slowed to an uneasy stillness again as Jemima swore under her breath.

'Did anyone feel a hole or crevice that it could've slipped into?'

The flat replies indicated not.

'It has to be here, it just has to,' Jemima repeated to herself, still groping the ground.

But it wasn't. The phone had vanished. They sat backed against the wall in a row, realising it provided their only orientation. The blackness was so dense, it had no beginning and no end.

'Ooh, I've got stomach cramps,' Millie groaned.

'It's okay, Mil,' Archie said, trying to quell his own panic. 'Don't work yourself up.'

'But I'm scared. We don't know what's down here,' she said, biting into her lip.

'There – is – nothing – down – here.' Oliver spoke each word emphatically to stress his conviction. 'If something *was* waiting to grab us, it would've happened by now.'

'Don't say things like that – you don't know anything about it! No-one even knows where we are!' Jemima said, scowling in his direction.

'*We* don't know where we are!' Millie added between short sharp breaths.

'Well, I'm not just sitting here in the dark. I'm heading back *now!*' Jemima began crawling, cautiously feeling her way along the stone slabs. 'Who's coming?' she said over her shoulder.

'Me,' said Millie, groping in the direction of Jemima's voice.

'Me too,' said Archie. 'But that's not the way back – it's this way.'

'What? No, it's this ... are you sure?' Jemima stopped and twisted around, feeling for the wall. She slumped against it again.

'Not absolutely, but I think ...' Archie's voice faded.

They fell into silence again; each gripped by a confusion that made breathing difficult. This was a new kind of fear – this total blackness made space and direction unknowable.

'This is beyond a nightmare! The phone's vanished. It's pitch black, and we don't even know which way's which!' Jemima sighed heavily. 'Maybe two go one way, and two ...'

'No, we have to stay together. Please!' Millie stretched her hand out to clutch Jemima's arm but she was out of reach. She pulled it back quickly as if it might be snatched by the darkness.

'Okay ...' Archie said from the opposite direction. He sounded further away from them. 'The stone floor sort of changes just over here. The ground's more like compacted earth this way, and the wall's veering slightly. Actually, it's swinging quite sharply now. It could mean something ...' his voice tapered off.

The others moved slowly towards him, groping their way along the wall as it changed direction, aware that the sandstone blocks had changed to a smooth rock face.

'And wait, I think ... I see something.' Archie had stopped. 'Can you see it? Straight ahead, can you see it?' he repeated as the others reached him. 'Just a pinprick – a speck?'

'No, you're imagining it.'

'Yes, I do ... a faint dot ... I think.'

'It may be a shaft from above,' Archie suggested, continuing to feel his way with the others following. 'Or it could be the far end of the tunnel ...'

The passageway had become more cave-like; the space above their heads seemed to have opened up a little.

'Or the beginning', Millie added in a lighter tone, reaching up to the ceiling and trying to straighten her back. As she did, she let out a piercing scream, her arms flailing above her head.

'What the … What!'

'There's something … ugh … up there.' She fell against her cousin. 'Something long 'n thin … flicked … out at me,' she stammered, shaking uncontrollably. 'I think it's a …'

They all recoiled against the wall, straining to see into the black void above.

'Okay, shh … stay still … There's a bit of light now … just let your eyes adjust,' Archie whispered, trying to sound composed.

No-one moved. Gradually a snake-like form came into focus, suspended into the passage from a darker cavity above. Its long body coiled back on itself, poised ready to strike. Still no-one moved. Moments passed, but the creature also hung motionless, mirroring their rigid stares. They stayed glued against the wall, barely breathing, eyes cemented on the creature, watching for the slightest move, for signs of attack.

Finally, in a voice barely audible, Millie stuttered, 'You know, maybe … maybe it's not … alive. Maybe I just hit my hand against it. Maybe, it's not …'

'Okay, just wait,' Archie said, slowly taking off his polo shirt and wrapping it around his hand.

He stepped towards the coiled creature and reached out with his covered arm. The serpent didn't flinch. Archie edged closer, flicking it with his shirt. It didn't react. He threw the fabric over it and it hung suspended from the rigid form.

'It's a tree root,' Oliver declared, as if he'd known all along.

The others exhaled loudly, coming forwards for a closer look.

'I'm sorry.' Millie felt mortified. Jemima touched her shoulder reassuringly, but she squealed in fright again, making them all laugh this time.

'Okay, come on. What're we waiting for? Let's go,' urged Oliver, moving to take the lead. 'We'll be fine now if we keep heading this way.'

'Oh, you're the big hero now, are you? Going to save us all from the mess you got us into, are you?' Jemima chided but they all laughed again, though Oliver said nothing more.

They continued in the direction of the glimmer, still feeling their way along the walls. Eventually, as the light became stronger, shadows began to form around them, throwing up grotesque shapes on the overhead cavity. They could make out moss and lichen growing high up between cracks as the passageway became more cavern-like. They breathed its earthiness with relief. The cavity ahead began tapering towards a distinct sliver of light, indicating its narrow exit. Jemima, now in the lead, held up her hand to halt the others, pointing to thick tree roots jutting from the ground across their path.

'Careful here. We'll have to go single file through this bit,' she said. 'And just remember, we don't know where this comes out.'

'Yeah, could be a smugglers' den,' said Millie, grinning and elbowing her brother.

'Ha-ha, very funny, Mil,' Oliver replied, relieved the tension was lifting.

'Okay, stay close when we get outside,' Jemima continued, 'and keep your voices low. It may be private property or something.'

'Yeah, we could come out in an old warehouse or disused depot.'

'And yeah, with a barbed-wire fence and vicious guard dogs.'

'It could be used by criminals as a secret hideout.'

'Trust you lot to think of that!'

The banter kept them busy as they continued single file towards the increasing light.

'Anyway,' said Millie, 'anywhere's better than being stuck in this tunnel.'

Yep, thought Archie.

As the space widened slightly again, it became obvious they were now inside a deep natural rock formation. They'd have to squeeze sideways to get through to what appeared to be the mouth of the cave, then edge their way around and over large loose boulders to scramble outside. After the gloom of the tunnel, they were already squinting against the brightness.

'Ahh, I can feel a breeze, and smell the gum leaves!'

'It looks like the entrance is hidden by boulders,' Oliver piped up from behind, as they saw the opening framed by rocks beyond. 'I'll go first,' he yelled, edging past them.

'Shh,' Jemima hissed as she turned with her finger pressed to her lip. 'I'll ...'

But ignoring her, Oliver was already skirting around her to clamber across the boulders ahead.

'Don't go charging out ...' she called. But he was gone, out of sight behind a stand of rocks.

The others quickened their pace to follow him, picking their way hurriedly across the rocks to catch up. Then came a hair-raising shriek.

****

Chapter 4

Where on Earth?

'What the …?' Archie sprang forwards, dodging the edge of a massive rock, narrowing his eyes against the brightness, before coming to an abrupt stop.

Oliver was slumped on the ground, bent double.

'Ahh!' he yelled again, clutching his foot.

Millie and Jemima came around the corner, almost stumbling into his bent body as their eyes adjusted to the light.

'Far out, Ollie! What now? What happened?' his sister wailed.

Jemima just glared down at him.

'It's my ankle. It's not my fault,' he groaned. 'The rocks were wobbly and I couldn't see. I just folded.' He pushed himself up onto an elbow, but rocked back and forth.

'Geez, mate!' said Archie, as he dropped next to him. 'Do you think it's broken?'

'Don't know … don't think so. Can you help me get … this shoe off? Ahh!'

Jemima was finding it difficult to show sympathy. She suspected he was making more of it to distract from his blunder. She looked across at Millie and shook her head.

'Just as well it's not fatal, seeing we don't have a body bag!' she said, lowering herself onto a flat rock.

Oliver threw her a look that said *Not funny*, before re-examining his ankle in a more composed fashion. Millie and Archie sat on the ground beside him. His injury had allowed them time to take in their immediate surrounds, but large rocks and dense foliage restricted their view beyond the area around the cave's entrance. From where they sat, its entrance was concealed behind a rock wall covered in trailing plants and thick rambling vines.

Where on earth?

Jemima leaned back along the rock and tilted her head towards the sky. It felt good to stretch after being hunched in the tunnel. A lone black bird glided across the blue expanse letting out a lazy, drawn-out *kaa, kaa, kaa-aa*. She narrowed her eyes against the brightness, wishing she had her sunnies.

'Where on earth are we, anyway?' said Millie.

A flock of noisy rainbow lorikeets settled in the trees overhead, screeching excitedly as if competing to provide Millie with an answer. Then, changing their minds, they took off, leaving the foliage to scatter its vanilla scent from fluffy blossoms.

'Not sure, but it's a great spot,' Jemima said, breathing in the fragrance, and deciding she'd bring her boyfriend here for a picnic. 'We must be in Barangaroo Reserve, I s'pose,' she added, squinting into the treetops. Then, with a smirk, she continued, 'But clearly no-one's within earshot or they'd 've heard your carry-on, Ollie. You sounded like you were being murdered.'

Oliver, still examining his foot, ignored the remark.

Archie walked to the edge of the clearing and peered between the stand of rocks. 'I don't remember thick bush like this at Barangaroo. It's pretty dense,' he called over his shoulder.

Jemima joined him, shielding her eyes as she scanned the bush. 'Yeah, this doesn't look familiar.'

'I can smell smoke, just faintly. But the sky's so clear. So, where the hell are we?'

At the mention of smoke, Oliver reached into the pocket of his cargo shorts for his inhaler, thinking at the same time he'd check Google Maps. But scowls from the others reminded him he had neither phone nor puffer. 'Oh ...' he said, turning his gaze away. 'Well, that's not *all* my fault.'

'We must be in some reserve or park, going by all the bird sounds,' said Millie as a magpie started up its pleasant warble from a nearby branch.

'Actually, it's the *lack* of sound that's weird,' Jemima said as the birdsong faded. 'I can't hear *any* traffic noise. Not even in the distance, can you?' she asked, tilting her head.

'No. That's odd, cos we can't be far from Windmill Street. We weren't in the tunnel all *that* long,' replied Millie.

'Well, come on; let's check it out,' said Archie. 'Someone wait here with Ollie.'

'No, I'm coming.' Oliver groaned, struggling to his feet.

'Lean on me then, cuz,' said Archie, taking Oliver's weight against him. 'Okay?'

'Yep,' Oliver replied. 'The sooner we work out where we are, the sooner we can head back home.'

'As long as it's *above* ground – I'm not going back in there,' Archie said under his breath, glancing back to the cave.

As they emerged from the clearing, their view was still somewhat restricted by forest, with an understorey of tree ferns and sprawling bushes, but they could see that the ground sloped gently away from them and they could hear water somewhere below.

'Which way d'you reckon? We still don't know if this is private property.'

'Well, keep your voices down till we do,' Jemima directed, stepping over a fallen moss-covered tree trunk to lead the way. 'Let's head to the water. When we see the Harbour Bridge, we'll get our bearings.'

Oliver limped along with Archie's help, huffing and puffing but without complaint until the grade became too steep.

'I'll have to sit, guys,' he panted, dropping onto a low rock. 'You go on; I'll wait here.'

Millie opened her mouth but Oliver put up his hand.

'I'm okay, Mil.'

As Jemima led the way further downhill, they debated their whereabouts in relation to the Harbour Bridge.

Millie peered through the trees towards the water. 'We should see it, like, any second.'

'But if the tunnel came out at Barangaroo, we're heading away from the bridge, aren't we? Which would mean Circular Quay's behind us, right? Anyway, we'll know soon enough.'

Their pace slowed as they approached the shoreline and emerged onto a small empty beach. Waves lapped gently against the sand but there were no paved walkways along the foreshore, no watercraft bobbing in the harbour ahead of them. There were no shops, office buildings or apartment blocks in view. And there was no imposing bridge spanning the harbour.

No-one spoke as they scanned in every direction, staring across the expanse in search of a landmark. But, even in the distance, there were no skyscrapers, no ferries crossing the harbour … nothing but forest edging the water as far as they could see. For a second, Archie thought he saw canoes pulled up on the far shore, but realised they were fallen logs. Though curling wisps of smoke rose in the distance, there was no sign of life. Only the water moved. Without a word they plonked themselves in a row on a flat rock shelf that jutted over the water.

'Okay, this is spooky,' Jemima finally uttered their thoughts. 'Where is everyone?'

With no obvious explanation they sat in silence, each hoping a group of bushwalkers would come sauntering around the corner, or a car alarm or siren would suddenly ring out.

'Well, maybe somehow the tunnel went *under* the harbour and we've come out in a national park?' Millie ventured, aiming to sound upbeat. 'Or maybe we're on one of the harbour islands?'

'Yeah, but we'd still see houses across the water. We'd still see yachts and ferries. Come to think of it, I haven't even heard a plane since we've been out of the tunnel.'

Millie didn't reply, instead biting nervously into her top lip. Archie sat looking over the water, slowly scrunching dried leaves....

'I don't get it.' Jemima shook her head slowly. A light breeze wafted across the water, making her shiver despite the warmth of the afternoon. She scanned the harbour again but saw only forest.

'Let's go back,' said Archie, scrambling to his feet. They

retraced their steps and as they approached Oliver, he flapped his arm, indicating for them to keep quiet. He clearly had news to share.

'Did you hear it? From back that way,' he whispered, pointing over his shoulder. 'Sounded like someone shouting orders! Like soldiers – in the distance. This could be ADF land.'

'Australian Defence Force? That's a relief, I suppose.' Archie paused to listen. 'Can't hear a thing now. Actually, that means it's a restricted area, doesn't it? We shouldn't be here!'

'And it still doesn't tell us where we are? It doesn't make sense so close to the city.'

'What city? We're in the middle of no-where!'

'Okay, there has to be a logical way to work this out,' said Ollie, shuffling his position to reach for a stick. Picking it up, he drew a line across a patch of bare ground in front of him. 'Let's say the tunnel came out *near* Barangaroo.' He added a curve to show the waterline.

'I know it changed direction,' he said, raising a hand to ward off interruption. 'But we must be west of the bridge. Somewhere about here.' He jabbed his map.

'So, if we follow the shoreline round to our right ...' Archie took over, drawing an extended line on Oliver's map with his own stick. 'We'll *have* to come to Circular Quay ... sooner or later.'

'Wouldn't it be better to go to the top of the ridge behind us first to get a better view?' said Millie, looking up the slope behind Oliver. 'And that's the direction the voices came from.'

'Okay, let's head that way ... Sooner or later we have to see somewhere familiar.'

'I hope so. This's pretty scary,' said Millie, looking around.

'Yeah.' Oliver huffed to his feet. 'I was thinking we could be the only survivors ... Did you see that movie about some people being the only ones left after ...?'

'Oh shut it, Ollie! And keep your voice down, will you.'

'I meant there might be snakes 'n stuff,' said Millie, taking wary steps. 'I don't like walking through long grass. There could be ...' She let out a sudden shriek, flapping her hands around her face.

'It's just a native wasp, Mil,' said Jemima. 'It'll leave you alone if you stop swiping at it. Same with snakes ... just stamp your feet as you walk.' She demonstrated with heavy steps.

'Yeah, the vibration warns them off before you're anywhere near them,' Archie added.

'It's okay for you two. You lived near the bush,' said Millie, embarrassed by her display. 'You still wanna be a ranger, Jem?' she asked, deflecting attention from it.

'Probably not now ... I'd rather do something that pays well without a lot of effort,' Jemima said, laughing. 'Oh, look at that,' she said, pointing to a butterfly hovering above feathery blossoms. 'See the orange and blue spots along its wings. I've never seen anything like that, have you?'

But Millie, intent on scanning the ground ahead, hadn't noticed. Their conversation led them uphill through thickly timbered forest that became more open as they neared the ridge. By the time they reached the summit, they were all breathless and came to a halt as harsh orders drifted from the other side of the hill. They darted behind a bush amid Ollie's stifled groans, then cautiously peeped over the crest towards the cove below.

'I see rooftops down that way,' said Oliver squinting. 'They're just huts though.'

Millie pointed down the slope. 'See there ... movement by the water ... and an old sailing ship?' She turned to the others with a puzzled expression.

'Listen.' Archie put up his hand. 'The voices – they're coming from that way.' He nodded to the far right below them. 'And I can just make out some guys in red jackets. See, down there?'

'Red jackets? Sailing ship? It *must* be a re-enactment then, or a movie set. So, where are we?' Jemima looked back at where they'd come from, then across the water in front of them.

'We must be further from the city than we thought, cos this

should be Circular Quay?'

'So … *where* are we?' Jemima repeated in a harsh, impatient tone.

Millie let out a gasp. As they turned to her, her hand went to her chest. Her eyes looked enormous against her drained complexion. Her face had taken on a chilling expression. 'It's impossible but … but,' she stuttered looking back to the bay.

'What?' The others stared at her as if she'd gone mad.

'What do you mean?' Jemima demanded.

'Look over there.' Millie pointed across the cove in front of them. 'That's where the Opera House *should* be … This *is* Circular Quay!'

There was a long silence as they tried to grasp her meaning.

'What? … But …' Jemima whispered, turning a horrified gaze towards the sailing ship. 'It's not *where* we are?' She faltered, trying to form an explanation. 'It's *when* …' Her voice trailed off as she dropped to her knees, cupping her hands around her mouth to stifle the shock.

****

Chapter 5

Reality Dawns

'How's this poss ... possib ...' Jemima swallowed and tried again, but her tongue wouldn't form the word. Her mind raced, her arms felt weak. She turned to the others crouched on the ground beside her, hoping that perhaps this was an elaborate joke. But their pale, pinched faces mirrored her fear and confusion. She closed her eyes, trying to fight the panic, searching for a logical explanation, but all she managed to splutter was, 'I don't get it.'

Cruel laughter from the camp below drifted across her words like a taunt, as if it were some kind of dare. From their hiding spot they peered through the foliage down to the cove as another harsh order echoed across the water. They scrambled forwards for a better view, hoping it would solve their confusion.

The sailing ship they'd spotted as they came over the hill was anchored close to a timber wharf on the far bank. Near the quayside, a blacksmith's forge discharged a steady metallic clang that resonated across the water. From this angle they could see men rolling barrels and stacking boxes as guards pointed and jabbed with jerky, hostile movements. Small storehouses stood near the pier and, beyond them, a wide track led to a two-storey building that dominated the opposite shore. It looked out of place, as if it had been plonked onto the landscape as part of a movie set.

'That's the governor's house, I suppose,' Millie muttered, trying to make sense of the scene.

Sentry boxes flanked its entrance and guards in red jackets paced back and forth along the fenced perimeter. To its left, a line of Monopoly-shaped bark huts spread across the hillside, surrounded by cleared ground littered with tree stumps. Smaller whitewashed huts sat nearer the waterline where a British flag fluttered atop a tall pole. The scene looked at odds with its backdrop of majestic forest.

Along one edge of woodland, they could now make out groups of men chopping and felling more trees, carving further openings into the wilderness. Across the distance they could see some workers dragging their feet, their movement hampered by leg irons. Others had chains hanging between their wrists. Millie put a hand across her mouth to muffle a groan while the others stared in horror. No-one spoke as they each tried to adjust to the strange reality that was unfolding. Millie was right. Impossible as it seemed, they'd gone back in time – to the convict settlement in Sydney Cove. It was unbelievable, but the evidence was all around them.

It was a lot to take in – far too much to put into words – so they sat in silence watching the softening sunlight reflected across the water and listening, between the intermittent yelling and clanking of metal, to the swish and slap as the tide licked the rocks along the shoreline. The cove shimmered with silvery flecks that dipped and curved across its surface, like gently swaying velvet, suspended between its shores. It could have been a peaceful scene but for the other frightening reminders of their bizarre and alarming situation: the aggressive voices, the forced labour, the chains. They sat in their concealed location for a long time, silently trying to process their dilemma.

Soon, the afternoon chatter of birds was threaded with domestic sounds carried on the breeze: female voices calling, dogs barking, and childish shrieking. The workday seemed to be winding down. Below them, where the vegetation thinned closer to the shore, they could see the roofs of huts, some with stone chimneys releasing wisps of smoke. Closer and down to their left, some sort of building work was going on near the waterfront. Between the trees they could make out a cart pulling away from the site amid billows of dust that told them a track ran parallel to the waterline. As the cart rumbled along they could see it was men – not horses or oxen – straining to pull its weight.

'What're we doing here?' Archie said at last.

No-one responded. A rock-wallaby hopped deftly between clumps of grass nearby, without attracting attention. They just sat dazed, each still immersed in feelings of what this meant.

'It must've been a tesseract tunnel ...' Oliver mumbled, thinking aloud as he rubbed his ankle.

'What? Oh, you and your movies, Ollie! Now's not the time ...'

'I'm not talking about a movie,' Oliver snapped. 'And this is about time, isn't it?' His attitude made the others look up in surprise; it was out of character for him to react in such a serious manner. 'Tesseract's a scientific thing – another dimension – like space-time.'

'Well, I've never heard of a tesseract tunnel.'

'That's cos I made that bit up,' he retorted, 'but other dimensions exist, you know. The world we see every day – our three-dimensional one – isn't the full story, Jem.' He glared at his cousin, expecting another chiding, but Jemima looked away and they all fell into another sullen silence.

'Not many people about now,' said Archie, noticing the workers had gone. 'I suppose there's a curfew when their day's work's all done.'

'Yeah, and we can't stay here hiding forever,' Jemima added. 'We have to get moving.'

'No, I don't want to ... not yet,' Millie blurted. Her eyes were wide with fear. 'This place is full of evil criminals, sent here cos of the terrible stuff they've done. It's not safe to move, not yet.'

'Okay, you stay here with Ollie, then,' said Archie. 'And we'll ...'

'No, no, we should stay together. Safety in numbers and all that.'

'Why don't we just retrace our way back to the tunnel?' Oliver suggested. 'And maybe ...'

'No, that won't be as easy as it sounds – it's late arvo already. It could be dark before we find the tunnel again – especially the way your ankle's looking now, Ollie. You okay to move, Ol?', said Jemima.

'Yep.' Oliver clambered to his feet, determined to keep up.

'I don't think we should get any closer to the settlement', said Archie, 'Let's go towards the headland which seems more secluded.'

Jemima and Oliver's nods signalled agreement and they started to move when ...

'Yeah, but hang on,' said Millie, holding back. 'Before we go anywhere, we need to sort out what to say if ... you know. I mean, look at us ... How do we explain being here?'

'We won't have to say anything if we stay out of sight, Mil. Luckily we're not wearing bright stuff,' Jemima whispered back.

As they made their way across and downhill, clambering between boulders trying to stay hidden, voices in conversation became more distinct. By the time they were close enough to observe the meeting by the water, they were near the end of the peninsula, some distance from the main settlement. They found a concealed vantage point on a level rock shelf but stayed huddled behind bushes to observe the goings-on.

This is such a lovely spot, thought Jemima as diagonal rays of light intensified the shades of green spilling down the slope: olive greens, blue greens and lush lime-green leaves tipped with crimson, threaded together like a patchwork quilt.

Below they could see a group gathered on a wide rock platform elevated above the water's edge. A small building with a cone shape jutting from its roof partially blocked their view. But they could see people congregated around a small fire – some sitting, some standing. The focus seemed to be a group of three at the centre. A burst of laughter erupted from the group. It wasn't malicious laughter; it was the sound of shared enjoyment. Millie turned to the others in relief.

'It's something to do with that guy with his back to us; he's jotting something on paper. See? The one in a lightish shirt, with a plait down his neck.'

'And the young couple next to him, they're Kooris.'

'All the others ... are Koori too,' said Archie, scanning the scene.

32

'Looks like we'll fit ...' Jemima put a hand up, puckering her lips to shush him.

'What's the whitefella saying?' she said softly, tilting her head. 'Sounds like the same phrase over and over. They're trying to teach him something. They laugh and repeat it, and he tries it again and then writes in his book.'

'Ben-ne-long ...' The word began a sentence that floated up to them as if in a speech bubble. Another bout of laughter erupted.

'Bennelong?' Millie repeated with a jolt. 'He was a young warrior that came to live in Sydney Cove.' She cast her eyes over the area to get her bearings.

The others, taken by her intensity, watched her.

'So ... somewhere around here ...' she said, still looking about, 'is where the south pylon of the Harbour Bridge stands, isn't it?' Not waiting for a reply, she continued. 'So that spot must be Dawes Point,' she said, pointing to the meeting place below. 'Cos like I said, the Opera ...'

'It *is* Dawes Point,' said a voice from behind.

They jumped and spun around like puppets in a line. The boy looking at them from a ledge above appeared to be a little older than Oliver. He wore a blue jacket and spoke his words distinctly. His dark face surveyed them with curiosity. 'This place is also Tar-Ra,' he added with a nod towards Millie. 'You called those people *Koori*,' he said, glancing at the meeting place below them. '*My* people are Gadigal.' He thumbed his chest, then looking from one to the other, he asked, 'But who are *you*?

****

33

Chapter 6

Adjustment

'Um … who are we?' Archie tried to stall his reply while his thoughts raced. They were utterly unprepared for such a question. They should've discussed their spiel about what they're doing here. *The fact is*, he thought, *we don't know*. The others were looking at him, waiting for him to continue, but he was completely tongue-tied; his initial 'um' had erupted from his lips involuntarily.

'Um,' Jemima took over.' We're a bit lost, actually. We are from over that way,' she said, pointing towards the crest. 'But we, um, don't know how to get back … and, um, our friend here has hurt his foot.'

All eyes went to Oliver.

'Surgeon White will treat it. I will take you to him.' The boy spoke very formally, saying each word slowly and precisely.

'Oh no … thank you.' Jemima spoke in a panicky voice, realising the danger of drawing any further attention to their presence. 'We just need to get back home. We just need somewhere for him to rest a while and then we'll go home … um, tomorrow.'

The boy once again looked them over, one by one. His manner told them he was wary of their unexplained arrival.

'I know you are not from here,' he said, addressing each of them with a slight nod. 'But are you *con-victs*?' He said the final word as two distinct syllables.

'No!' They all reacted in unison.

Their shocked response seemed to convince their observer that they were not – and that they were genuinely lost. He jumped from the ledge to their level and crouched next to Oliver to inspect his injured ankle. As he stood, a movement near the track below caught all their attention. A man in uniform was sauntering towards the social gathering on the rock platform at Dawes Point, which, by now, was winding up.

'That is Lieutenant Tench,' the boy said, following their gaze. 'He visits Mr Dawes when he is off duty. He writes a journal about *everything* happening in this place.'

'Well, *we* can't end up in his journal!' Millie blurted. 'He can't know we are here!' she added urgently. 'Nobody can …' Her words petered out, but her eyes were pleading.

The boy watched her with a penetrating expression.

After a pause he said, 'I will help you. Wait here.' Then, as deftly as he'd appeared, he was gone.

'Do you think we can trust him?' Oliver said when he was out of earshot. 'He might've gone to get soldiers.'

'Do we actually have a choice?' said Jemima, her hands spread. 'It's getting late; *you* can't go anywhere fast on that foot. Even if you could, we have no idea *where* to go.'

'Why does he talk and act so funny?' Millie said to no-one in particular.

'I'm sure he's thinking the same about us,' said Archie, indicating their clothes.

Millie looked down at her polo shirt, shorts and runners, then across at the others' similar get-ups.

'We don't exactly blend in here – especially you Jem,' Archie pointed out.

Jemima fingered her loopy silver earrings. She undid the clasps and dropped them into her pocket but decided it was too fiddly to remove the brow piercings. Nothing could be done about her tattoo and shaved head. *We'll be home before anyone else sees us*, she told herself.

'And your braces, Ol,' Millie whispered. 'You'll have to keep your mouth shut.' She met Jemima's gaze and exchanged a quick smile at her unintended wisecrack.

But Oliver didn't notice. He put his hand across his mouth, knowing they wouldn't be easily removed. He was about to respond

35

when movement and urgent-sounding conversation from below made them all freeze. The commotion came from further along the shoreline, from the direction they had come. They turned to peer down through the foliage as several canoes were dragged onto a strip of sand along the waterfront by several black men – all naked. Two others were helping a man out of a canoe. He was slumped over and holding his hand to his opposite shoulder, groaning with the pain of movement. Blood covered his upper body and left a trail on the sand as he moved forwards. The other men supported him as he staggered towards a long, low building. Then the group disappeared from view.

'He's been speared or shot,' Millie whispered. 'I'm really scared.'

No-one responded, they were all feeling the vulnerability of their situation: stuck in a place where misery and violence seemed the norm.

****

When the young stranger returned he was carrying a thick wad of bark and had a woven net bag draped over his shoulder. Millie wanted to ask about the injured man but decided against it.

'For you,' he said, kneeling next to Oliver. He unrolled the paperbark and laid it next to Oliver's grazed ankle, now double its usual size. He signalled for Oliver to lift his leg onto the bark and proceeded to cover it with damp leaves taken from his bag. They smelt strongly of tea-tree oil. After carefully wrapping the swollen area with soft bark, he tied it in place with twine, leaving the toes and ball of the foot exposed.

'Geez thanks, mate,' Oliver mumbled as the youth stood and faced the others.

'My name is Nanberry,' he said with another slight bow. 'Mr White wants my name to be Andrew Sneap Hamond Douglass White, but it is Nanberry.'

They smiled at his polite manner and formal English.

36

Adjustment

After they had each told him their name, he indicated for them to follow him back up the slope. Careful to stay out of sight, they traced their way between bushes and large rocks with Oliver supported between Archie and Jemima. Millie stayed close beside them where possible, glancing behind every few steps. No-one spoke until they were heading back down the other side of the ridge.

'This way,' Nanberry said simply, cutting across the slope and leading them into a small secluded clearing partially bounded by a curved rock overhang. 'You can stay here tonight,' he said. 'But no fire,' he pointed to the charcoal remnants of one.

The journey had taken only a few minutes so they knew they weren't far from the settlement.

'Okay, thanks, mate,' said Archie, helping Oliver lower himself against a tree before dropping next to him. The others, including Nanberry, sat on the ground in an arc facing them.

'What is *okay*? Nanberry asked. 'I have not heard this English word.'

'Oh, it means, *I agree* or *yes*. Something like that,' Archie replied.

'And *mate*? I hear the sailors say it but ...' Nanberry looked from one to the other.

'Um, it means *friend*.'

Nanberry nodded and smiled, taking the net bag from his shoulder. 'You need vittles, I think,' he said.

'*Vittles*? What's that?' Jemima asked. 'What does it mean?' she rephrased, mimicking his polite curiosity for unknown words.

Nanberry turned to her with a confused expression.

'It is English. You do not know *vittles*?' he asked, his brow creasing further.

'Er ... it means *food*, I think?' Millie offered, waiting for Nanberry to confirm with a nod. 'But we don't say that now ... I mean, we don't say it where we live.'

'You speak English but you are not British?' He was clearly baffled.

'Actually, our country is called Australia. It is different to this place … now.'

'I see,' he said looking thoughtful. Then, changing the subject, he turned to his net bag.

'I have only salt pork and biscuit for you … and water.' He laid a roundish, leather flask beside Archie. 'It is all I could manage.'

They nodded appreciatively as he unrolled a paperbark package containing four small portions of dried meat and some broken pieces of stiff crust. He laid the bark on the ground between them like a platter. It didn't look at all inviting but, suspecting it was all they'd get till the next day, they hesitantly bit into his offering. The meat was tough and stringy, the biscuit hard and tasteless, but they thanked him profusely

While they were eating, Nanberry walked to the edge of the clearing and began collecting armfuls of bracken fern, which he deposited beneath the rock overhang. He gestured, putting his hands next to his head, that they could be piled together and used as pillows. They nodded appreciatively.

'Thanks mate, for believing we are lost. I know we look … different,' said Archie, wishing he had a plausible story for their unexplained presence. Earlier, when Nanberry was leading them through the bush to their hiding place, Archie had wondered how he would've reacted in Nanberry's place. Again, he wondered *why* he was helping them.

As if he'd read Archie's thoughts, Nanberry looked from one to the other, then his features broke into a relaxed smile.

'Yes, you look different. I never saw a white woman in short trousers before … or …' He gestured to Oliver's braces and Jemima's brow studs. 'But …' he hesitated, tilting his head back to gaze up at the treetops. 'I saw many strange things when British came here.'

They nodded, feeling relieved by his acceptance of them. His smile broadened and then, deciding spontaneously to go into more detail, he sat between them again with legs crossed.

'When my people – called Gadigal – saw British ships coming,' he held his hand to shade his eyes as if peering across the ocean, 'they saw floating islands with great white wings. Then later they saw *many* new things come from those ships: animals with strange sounds, and many clever tools. And all the people had body coverings ... hiding them ... hiding all of them.' He chuckled, gesturing head to foot at his own clothes. 'They thought *Mee diee? – What are they? Are they men or women?* Those who came to meet our warriors showed only white faces ... smooth, no beard,' he explained. 'My people used signs and easy words to ask, *Mula ... gin?* That means *Man or Woman?* But they did not understand. Then one man got their meaning and dropped his trousers and they all laughed together.'

Nanberry's shoulders began shaking with amusement at the scene he was describing, and the others joined his infectious laughter. Encouraged, Nanberry rose from the ground and began to shuffle with short stiff steps as if in a straightjacket.

'Covered from their head to feet,' he repeated, enjoying the effect of his re-enactment.

'Yeah, they even wore hats and gloves,' Millie added.

Nanberry, still laughing, looked at her quizzically, wondering how she knew that.

'Shush, Mil,' said Jemima. 'Just let Nanberry tell the story, will you.'

Millie looked embarrassed and clamped her lips together. However, the distraction had changed the mood and Nanberry's face became thoughtful again. He gazed towards the forest.

'But when the white people set up camp, my people saw bad things: guns and chains and flogging. Then, one day, they saw something *more* terrible.'

'First, they heard drums beating to bring all the white people together in one place in Sydney Cove. Then they saw soldiers in red jackets bring one white man before the crowd – his hands and feet chained, like this.' Nanberry rose again and took restricted steps as if shackled with leg irons.

'My people watched – from behind trees like you – but they did not believe what their eyes saw. The soldiers took that man to a tree where there was a rope, like this.' He drew a loop in the air with his finger.

'A noose,' said Archie.

'Yes, a noose. They pushed him to climb to that place they call *gallows* – to stand before the noose. They put it around his neck and then ... they watched him hang till dead. They all just watched him.'

'My people said to their children, "Stay away from that place. Don't go near their camp."'

Nanberry paused as if deciding how much to say. 'But now I live in Sydney Cove.' He lifted his gaze and stared into the distance as if into his past, recalling a challenging experience.

Millie, like the others, wanted to ask questions but didn't interrupt.

'At first – like a bad dream – I did not understand what I saw. But ...' He gave a shrug and looked at each of them, giving his now-familiar nod. Then he stood abruptly as if noticing he was running late and addressed them as if talking to children. 'You must stay here,' he said, pointing to the ground, 'if you do not wish to be found. And you must leave before sunrise.'

'Thank you, Nanberry,' Millie said, feeling the words were not enough to express how grateful she was to him. 'Thank you for helping us,' she added awkwardly.

Nanberry nodded and paused as if he wanted to ask something, but didn't.

'Goodbye,' he said as he picked up his net bag and slung it over his shoulder. Seeing the panic on all four faces at his leaving, he added, 'I bid you well.' He gave another slight nod and he was gone.

The clearing fell into silence.

****

Chapter 7

Nanberry

Nanberry had felt their eyes on his back as he'd left the camp site. He could relate to their anxiety. Their sudden appearance had sparked memories of his own first impression of Sydney Cove.

At least *they* spoke a type of English. When he'd been brought in, he hadn't understood one word; he didn't know what the white men were thinking or planning. But he'd listened and worked out their meaning, and imitated their ways. His tongue had struggled with their sounds – especially *sh* and *ss* – but now the gov'nor called him 'a fine, clever lad'. Nanberry knew he was useful too; he was their interpreter, their go-between.

He scaled the ridgetop and peered down towards the hospital buildings, recalling his time there. It was where he'd first experienced the stuffy, stifling smell of their closed-in rooms – where he'd adjusted his fingers to hold a spoon the way they showed him and where, with difficulty, they'd guided his arms into a nightshirt for the very first time. And it was where, lying under the thing they called *blanket*, he'd gazed at the ceiling and felt a deep lonely confusion.

As he headed down the slope, he pulled at the buttons of his blue jacket. Though he'd come to understand the importance they placed on clothes, by the end of a day its tightness irritated him. But when Surgeon White's garden came into view, he was glad he'd left it on, knowing it pleased the doctor to see him dressed 'decently'.

White looked up and waved as Nanberry approached. 'There you are lad. Come tell me what I found today.' He waited till Nanberry was beside him before gesturing to his pile. 'Some sort of mushroom. How do you say it? *Gnal-lung-ul-la*?' Mr White stumbled through the sounds and Nanberry smiled at his attempt at the word.

'Yes, but those will give you sore belly.'

'Ah, just as well we are dining at the gov'nor's table tonight then.' He gave a deep chuckle and Nanberry followed him inside.

He was once again astounded that this clever man didn't know what he could and couldn't eat in the forest around him.

****

As he leaned over a bowl before the fire, washing his face with a warm cloth, Nanberry continued to ponder the mysterious appearance of the four young strangers. *Like fish out of water* ... that's what Surgeon White would say about them. That's what they had said about *him* when he'd gawked wide-eyed at all he saw in the Sydney settlement.

'You'll soon find your feet, lad', someone had said. And Nanberry – understanding only one of the words – had looked down at the boots hiding his toes. And when they'd laughed, he'd laughed with them.

But the four young arrivals – where had they come from? How did they get here? Not by sea ...

Their unexplained appearance today was nothing like the last influx of white strangers on the 'Second Fleet'. When the convicts were rowed ashore, the smell of them was gut churning; their faces were grey, their eyes sunken. Their bodies were caked in their own muck. Some had died as they were rowed ashore, or on the wharf as they were lifted out of the boats. He'd never seen the doctor so angry as when he spoke of the captain responsible for their misery.

'That monster should be hanged for his greed and cruelty,' he'd fumed. 'What they must've suffered!'

There'd been a flurry to pitch extra tents around the hospital for those with a chance of survival, and Surgeon White had asked Nanberry to go into the forest to collect more of the red gum to relieve their gut cramps, and wild greens to heal their wasted bodies.

By contrast, the four strangers Nanberry had met earlier didn't look starved or overworked. In fact, they looked better than any white person he'd seen in Sydney Cove. It wasn't surprising they were keen to get away. And they would be gone before sunrise, so there was no need to tell anyone – except maybe Boorong. She'd have helped them too when they'd said, 'No-one must know we are here.'

Nanberry looked across to where Mr White was sitting at the table, busily scrawling in his journal in the late-afternoon light. What would he make of the strangers' new words and peculiar dress? No doubt he would want to make a study of them, as he did with birds, fish and snakes.

****

Chapter 8

The Find

'What now?' said Millie after a long silence. The camp site seemed desolate without Nanberry.

'Well, I'm going to find a toilet spot while there's still some light. I don't want to go fumbling around in the dark later,' Jemima said decisively.

'Me too.' Millie jumped up to follow her beyond the edge of the clearing where diagonal shafts of light still streamed between the trees. They headed over to a stand of large rocks, with Millie clinging to Jemima's arm as they picked their way between tall ferns and grassy tussocks. The boys watched their forms fade into the forest and disappear behind the rocky outcrop.

****

'You're going to have to toughen up Mil,' Jemima whispered with an impatient edge as they headed back up the slope with Millie clutching tightly to her again. 'It's not critters you have to worry about here, you know.'

'Yeah, I know. I'm just not used to this ... I imagine things creeping through the long grass towards me – especially when I'm squatting!'

They both giggled at the memory of her attemping to balance while sitting on her haunches and trying to scan 360 degrees at the same time.

Becoming serious again, Jemima said, 'It's humans we have to worry about here – not critters.'

'And speaking of that, Jem, I was thinking before – maybe you should turn your t-shirt inside out. I think Nanberry was confused by it.' Millie pointed to the lettering printed across her cousin's front: *Silence is Complicit.*

'Oh yeah, I should've thought of that,' said Jemima, starting to do so as they continued walking. 'Yeah, I saw Nanberry looking at my Southern Cross too,' she said, touching her tattoo. 'He seemed taken with it. I can't hide that, but the shirt … good point.'

Pulling the t-shirt back over her head, and slipping her arms through, she stopped abruptly and put her hand up to halt her cousin. Something protruding from a low rock formation had caught her eye; it was flat and rectangular, and completely out of place in their surroundings. She crouched, putting her finger to her lip, then edged closer, peering around to ensure they were alone.

The item was some kind of bound notebook tucked between horizontal rocks on a ledge. The base rock butted up to a wall behind it. It was a natural formation but looked like the perfect writing spot, with a backrest and a view of the bush below. Another rock sat along the edge of the journal, keeping it in place, presumably to stop the pages blowing open.

Millie put her hand out to touch the journal, seeing a large feather protruding from the pages like a bookmark. She pulled the journal closer, flicking open the cover to read the scrawled lettering on the first page: *Lieutenant Watkin Tench.* Beneath the name, centred on the page, read:

A Complete Account of the Settlement at Port Jackson

She stared open-mouthed. 'Wow, it's Tench's notebook! You know, the guy Nanberry said was keeping a journal about stuff that happens here.' Millie turned a stunned gaze to Jemima. 'Why would he leave it here … out in the open like this?' She looked around nervously to see if it was a trap – as if he may suddenly appear in his red military jacket, grab them by the shoulders and march them back to the settlement.

'It's not exactly out in the open, Mil. He just forgot it, I s'pose,' Jemima replied in a cool, matter-of-fact tone that restored Millie's rattled nerves. 'Just leave it. Come on.'

Jemima started walking away but Millie hesitated, still gawking at the journal. Then, on a whim, she snatched it up, hugged it to her chest and trailed Jemima who, seeing it, gave her a look that said *You're crazy.*

'It must be where he goes to write – his quiet place, away from his soldier duties,' Millie mused. 'Anyway, he must be done for today ... and it'll be back before he knows it's gone.'

Archie and Oliver were peering anxiously down the slope when the girls emerged from the forest from a different approach, and the boys looked utterly relieved to see them. Spotting the journal, their expressions changed to bewilderment. Millie rushed to explain how they'd found it slotted between rocks.

'I know it's risky,' she said, reading their minds, 'but a bit of inside information won't go astray.'

'We'll be out of here first thing in the morning, so what's the point?' said Jemima with a dismissive shrug.

Millie ignored her; and sat cross-legged with the book on her lap and opened it. She saw now that the feather between the pages was a quill used for writing. The tip was dark stained but empty. *Maybe he went to get more ink*, she thought, *and he'll be back ... No, it's late already*, she reminded herself, *it'll be too dark for writing.*

She turned the pages filled with swirly writing too difficult to decipher. But the word *captive* jumped out at her under the date *31st December 1788*. She glanced over the page.

'Listen, this might be about Nanberry. It's about a native kidnapped at Manly Cove.'

The others, with nothing else to do, drew closer.

'Maybe Nanberry was *abducted*.' She hunched forwards to focus on the handwriting and began reading Tench's words, skipping those she couldn't make out:

> *The prisoner was fastened with ropes to the boat ... Seeing himself separated from his people, he let out piercing cries of distress ... On his arrival at Sydney, everyone gathered at*

the wharf to see him. He appeared to be about thirty years old …

'Okay, that's not Nanberry,' said Jemima. 'He's in his early teens. But keep reading. It must've been terrifying for the poor guy, whoever he was.'

'It'd be like getting captured by aliens,' said Oliver.

'Yeah, it says he was terrified and trembling.' Millie skimmed the page then paraphrased: 'They took him to the governor's two-storey house and led him into the dining room with all the officers gathered … It says his name was A-ra-ba-noo.'

'Geez,' said Oliver. 'He'd be wondering what's gunna happen to him.'

'Part of this page is crossed out, but listen!' Millie followed the words with her finger:

He was vastly frightened and would not eat anything … Then, after dinner, we learnt he'd thought we were going to eat … him.

Millie was pleased when the others reacted with disbelief.

'What! Arabanoo thought the *British* were cannibals?' Jemima had an intrigued expression. 'Well, that'd be embarrassing for them … to be thought so uncivilised.'

Millie nodded and ran her gaze down the page till she found a section where she could read most words:

After dinner they cut his hair and his beard … followed by his immersion in a tub of water and soap; after which a shirt, a jacket and a pair of trousers were put upon him …

'That must've felt so creepy … strangers' hands on him. Then dressing him up like them,' said Oliver.

Millie skimmed a few pages then looked up. 'It says his fear gradually wore away …'

'Yeah, well realising you *weren't* going to be eaten would help!' Archie cut in again, but the others shushed him and urged Millie to keep going, as the twilight was beginning to fade.

She summarised as she skimmed. 'It says he told them about

his customs and language ... blah-blah-blah.' She flicked through more pages before pausing at a subheading. 'Okay ... Something really bad happens while he's in Sydney.' She read:

> *April 1789*
>
> *A calamity was now observed among the natives. Reports came in of bodies in all the coves and inlets of the harbour ... Pustules, similar to smallpox, were thickly spread on their bodies ...*
>
> *We learnt that a family lay sick in a neighbouring cove, so the governor, attended by Arabanoo and a surgeon, went by boat to the spot ... Here they found an old man stretched out before a fire and a boy of nine or ten years old pouring water on his head from a shell ...*
>
> *Eruptions covered the poor boy from head to foot; and the old man was so weak it was difficult to get him into the boat. However, their weakness made them incapable of escape, and they quietly submitted to be taken away by us.*

'Geez,' piped Oliver. 'It would be like an alien abduction and you're too weak to fight 'em off.'

'Stop butting in, Ollie!'

'Keep reading, Mil. This could be Nanberry. What happened to them?'

'It says they were taken to the hospital, where Arabanoo stayed with them.' She continued:

> *... And by the soothing behaviour of our medical gentlemen, they appeared grateful at the change in their situation. However, sickness and hunger had exhausted the old man so much; there was little hope of his recovery ...*

'They'd be scared I reckon — captive to strange-looking aliens.' Oliver pulled a gruesome face. 'Remember they'd been told to stay away from Syd ...'.

'Oh shut up with your sci-fi alien obsession, Oliver. Just listen, will you!'

'At least Arabanoo was there to assure them they weren't going to be eaten,' Archie said with a grin. He was about to continue when Millie put up her hand.

'Look, we're running out of light so I'll skim this bit. It says the boy *Nanberry* ate the fish offered him. So this *is* about Nanberry! It's how he ended up staying in Sydney Cove … Listen.' She read:

> *… The tenderness and anxiety of the old man for the boy was very moving. Although barely able to raise his head … the man kept looking at his child … patting him gently on the chest … and with dying eyes, seemed to recommend him to our humanity and protection … The old man lived only a few hours …*

Millie felt her eyes smarting and her throat tightening but continued:

> *Nanberry was adopted by Mr. White, surgeon of the settlement, and became one of his household …*

'So, Nanberry's an orphan,' said Jemima in a quiet voice.

'Far out, it must've been a shock at first, living there …' Oliver dipped his head in the direction of the settlement. 'Everything being so different – like the food, for a start.' He pulled a face, remembering the salt pork and hard biscuit he'd forced down earlier. 'And seeing convicts in chains, not knowing the rules.'

'Don't forget the floggings and hangings,' said Archie.

Millie was holding the journal close to her face now, squinting at the writing as she flicked through the pages in the fading light.

'I want to know what happened to Arabanoo,' she said, running her finger down the pages trying to find mention of him. 'Here it is,' she said suddenly. Then, reading with difficulty and skipping some words:

> *May, 1789*
>
> *I feel all my readers will share my regret … at the loss of Arabanoo, who died of the small-pox after six days … During his sickness he showed entire confidence in us … swallowing medicine offered to him in the hope of bringing relief …*

Millie rubbed her eyes. 'Sorry, I can't read anymore.'

'Wow. So *he* died after helping save Nanberry. What a story.

I'm glad we know it.'

Millie closed the book and they sat in stillness for a moment.

'It could explain why Nanberry helped us,' said Archie after a while. 'He knows how it feels, being lost.'

'Well luckily we won't be here after first light tomorrow,' said Jemima.

'Speaking of light, I've got to get this back before it's gone,' said Millie, peering into the forest.

Archie opened his mouth to offer to go, but Jemima cut in.

'Come on, quick; I'll go with you, Mil.'

The sun was slipping behind the mountains, with only a pale pink glow lighting the western sky. Shadows merged across the ground as Jemima steered the way around the rocks across the escarpment. Millie was digging her nails into Jemima's arm again as they hurried towards the outcrop before pausing to get their bearings in the dwindling light.

'That's where it was,' Millie whispered, pointing ahead.

She was about to move forwards again when Jemima grabbed her shirt. Beyond the rocks where they'd found the journal, half hidden by bushes, they could just make out bodies close together. Jemima put her finger to her lip and squatted to pick up a rock, which she flung further down the slope. As it hit the ground with a thud a good distance from the couple, voices gasped, the bodies sprang apart and leapt to their feet, before taking off up the slope.

'Quick, give it to me.'

Jemima grabbed the journal before Millie could object to being left alone. Returning a moment later, she said in a serious tone: 'We've got to get out of here before first light; we're too close to the settlement. I doubt those two saw us, but come on let's go.'

****

Chapter 9

Night Sounds

'You forgot this,' said Oliver, holding up Tench's quill as the girls reached the camp site panting.

'Well, I'm not going back now,' Millie said, plonking herself next to him. 'Not after what we just saw. Anyway, we'll be long gone before he discovers it's missing.' She swivelled the feather between her finger and thumb, gazing towards the empty fireplace, as Jemima described how they'd disturbed the couple. After wisecracks from the boys, their conversation fell to an uneasy lull.

'So what now?' Millie knew it was a pointless question; they had no choice but to stay put. However, now they were all the more aware of their vulnerability, that someone could easily discover them. She scoured the camp surrounds. The foliage on the fringe of the clearing quivered as the breeze lifted. She sat absolutely still, watching the leaves droop and then lift again as if they were inhaling and exhaling into the space between them. *They are breathing,* she thought.

In a delayed reaction to Millie's question, Jemima let out a long sigh, looked up and shrugged. Archie shifted his position and Oliver rubbed at his ankle but no-one offered a suggestion. Then, as if to deliberately fill the silence, a kookaburra began a deep chortle from above. Others progressively joined in so that the low chuckling soon progressed into a chorus of wild cackling that sounded almost maniacal. The hooting and chortling kept going like uncontrollable laughter until gradually fading again to a single drawn-out *ha … ha … ha,* and all went quiet again. It seemed such a decisive declaration of the day's end that Millie couldn't help a chuckle coming to her own throat as a funny thought occurred to her.

'Imagine the people from the First Fleet hearing that cackling at

51

sundown for the first time and not knowing it's only a bunch of harmless, fluffy birds. Cos – for all they knew – they could've been vicious blood-sucking creatures.'

Quiet chuckles came from the others, but their features were becoming cloaked in darkness now.

The area covered by the rock overhang was wide enough for them to sit comfortably side by side, with their backs to the rock wall, looking westwards down the slope; they'd all stay dry even if it rained. The back of the shallow recess curved in an arc of smooth rock. Up high, lacy ferns sprouted and hung from cracks like decorations. Beyond the alcove, smooth rusty-pink trunks stood out from the darkness in an almost symmetrical arrangement. To the west, broken views of a distant horizon were visible through the trees, with a faint sliver of lilac outlining the ridge of the rugged Blue Mountains. The night was closing in on them and with it came an eerie orchestra of bush sounds; the chirping of insects formed a continuous backdrop to the whirring of cicadas, which increased and receded in waves. Millie was familiar with those sounds but they'd always been *outside*. She'd heard them from the safety of home, behind the protection of glass and insect screens. She'd never spent a night in the bush before. Now, a deep drawn-out *whoo-hoo, whoo-hoo* came over the insect drone. She looked up to check Jemima's reaction.

'It's just a boobook owl, Mil; it won't hurt you. It's much more interested in those insects.'

Millie scanned the treetops for spooky owl eyes staring down at her.

'And it's probably not even close – their calls travel a long way,' Jemima added, seeing Millie's body language.

'But owls *are* spooky. Think Halloween. That's why they freak me ...' Oliver chipped in, but his words were cut short by a low breathy growl from the darkness just beyond the clearing. He hunched his shoulders as the back of his neck began tingling.

Millie pressed herself to the wall with a whimper. She tried to gauge Jemima and Archie's response, but couldn't see their faces. The growl came again, sounding closer and more sinister.

'What the hell is it? It sounds like a vampire wanting to suck my blood,' Oliver whispered as it came again: a deep husky meaningful snarl.

Then, what seemed like a muffled laugh erupted from Jemima.

'See, this is an example of what you said before Mil – how something can terrify us when we don't even know what it is. So go on – guess what's making that growl?' She was enjoying the suspense.

'I have absolutely *no* idea. I just want it to go away! … there it goes again.'

Wanting to ease their panic, Archie jumped in before Jemima could draw the tension out any further. 'It's just a possum, a common brush-tail trying to attract a mate,' he said, without looking at Jemima.

'You're *kidding* me? Geez, imagine being stuck here and *not* knowing that! You'd keel over from heart failure! See, they *are* dangerous,' Oliver said, turning to his sister, who thumped his shoulder.

The possum growled again and Millie said, 'It's still the freakiest sound I've ever heard.'

'I wish I had some insect repellent.' Archie swatted something crawling up his arm.

'I wish I had my pillow,' said Oliver.

'Yeah, and I bet, like the rest of us, you wish you had your phone, don't you?' Jemima said in an accusing tone. She was suddenly in a bad mood. 'Without a phone there's nothing!' She went on: 'No music, no video, no apps, no games, no photos, no chat, no nothin'! We're so completely cut off!'

'Well, just be grateful it's only one night of your life, Jem. We'll be home tomorrow and it'll all seem like a dream. Be thankful you don't live here all the time.' After a pause he continued, 'Actually, I meant to say before – we don't know what year this is, do we?'

Millie said immediately, '1791. I saw it in Tench's journal, with mostly blank pages after it.'

'Wow, so more than two hundred years in the past!'

'Stop it! You're freaking me out. I don't want to think about it,' Jemima said, putting her hands over her ears. *I wish I had my earpods*, she thought, clenching her jaw.

'What do we do now? Do you think we should take turns, you know, keeping a lookout?'

'A lookout for what?' said Oliver. 'If anyone *did* come prowling, what'd we do, anyway?'

'Well, we could all run and leave you as the bait!' Jemima said with a smirk.

'Huh, you're hilarious, Jem,' Oliver replied but the banter had lightened the mood so he continued: 'That salted pork Nanberry brought was awful, wasn't it? And I thought I was gunna break my teeth on the biscuit. He probably thought it's what we *usually* eat, thinking we're British. Good on him though cos it's gunna be a long night.'

'At least it's not cold. S'pose we'll have to sleep sitting up against the wall,' said Millie.

'Getting back to what you said before, Mil, I think we *should* take turns keeping a lookout. It'd just feel better ...' said Archie. 'I'll do the first stint, if you ...'

'It's way too early to think about sleep,' said Jemima, as if deciding for all of them.

'Not for me; I'm pooped,' Oliver said, leaning against the wall and stretching his arms in an exaggerated yawn.

Seeing her brother's eyes close, Millie realised she too felt wrecked by the day. *Was it only this morning I woke up to the drone of city traffic? What a day!* she thought, allowing herself to slump against Oliver, who then shifted himself sideways onto Nanberry's pile of bracken fern. She had no intention of sleeping just yet, but it was comforting leaning against her brother. She wondered if their mother would be worried yet ...

Night Sounds

Archie sat staring into the darkness, aware of Jemima's wide-awakeness but not knowing what to say. He knew his sister was the stronger of them. She was the cool one. He wished he had her boldness. He was more like his dad – laidback – that's how he'd describe it. But his mum had used the words 'apathetic and indifferent' against her husband during their yelling matches. Archie pushed the image away.

'Well, this is weird,' Jemima finally said without looking at him.

'It is what it is, I guess,' he said, realising he'd used his father's expression. His sister gave a short huff and he imagined her tight smile. 'It's true,' he said with a shrug. *Another of Dad's habits*, he thought, shifting his position to sit beside an already-snoozing Oliver, with Millie quietly collapsed against him.

'How can they sleep this early?' Jemima snapped.

'It's been a big day,' Archie said, stretching.

'Well, I'm wide awake, so I guess I'll do the first watch,' she said with a deep sigh.

At first he thought she was being sarcastic but he watched her pick up a short stick, brush aside the leaves and begin doodling in the earth beside her. He was surprised to hear her humming.

'No, it's okay Jem; I'm not tired enough to sleep yet.' It was the last thing Archie remembered.

****

Chapter 10

Strangers

'Are they dead?' Archie heard the words floating, as if through a dark tunnel. He tried to move but his arms felt numb.

'Get back quick – one of 'em stirred,' another voice came in a raspy whisper.

Archie kept his eyes closed, trying to decide if it was a dream, struggling to get his bearings.

'They must be foreigners from that place beyond the mountains? You know, where they say copper-skinned people get by with little work. They must be, cos look at them hands – never done a day's work in their lives, any of 'em, I'd say. Ee, they're odd looking, alright.'

Archie managed to push himself onto his elbow, aware of his pounding heartbeat and the smell of charcoal. *Ugh, I must've rolled near the fireplace*, he thought as memories came flooding back. He cracked an eyelid open. A face came close, female features peering into his. It wasn't Millie, or Jemima.

'What the ...?' He heard his voice slurring as he tried to focus, squinting into the glare. 'What? Who're you?'

Now the stranger's thin face was close enough that he could smell her sour breath and a strong whiff of stale sweat.

'That's what we're asking *you*!' she said in an aggressive manner.

There was another younger woman standing, hands on her hips, behind her, and a boy with his mouth agape, staring at him. They were all barefoot, their clothes ragged-looking.

'Okay, no need to yell,' said Archie, matching her hostile tone and looking over his shoulder. The others were still asleep, slumped along the rock wall, though he wondered how. He scrambled to a seated position, at the same time trying to figure out what to say.

'We're just sleeping. Not doing any harm to anyone.' He rubbed his eyes, realising it was *way* past sunrise. They should've left hours ago.

'Well, how come we ain't seen youse before?' the spokeswoman asked, narrowing her eyes. 'Youse didn't come on the fleet, cos we know everyone here.'

'Because we're not from round here – we've lost our way.' Archie used a softer tone, hoping to appeal to their pity, or maybe their curiosity. It seemed to work because the young woman sat down near him, waiting for him to continue. The other two did the same.

'Go on then,' she whispered, as if they were now part of a conspiracy. 'Youse from that place beyond them Blue Mountains, then?' She nodded to the west. 'Heard stories 'bout that place, we have.'

The other two continued staring.

'Er, maybe.' He thought it best to be elusive. He was deciding how to continue when Oliver grunted and stretched, disturbing the girls sprawled either side of him.

'What's going on?' Jemima said, running her fingers through the curly half of her head. Then, guarding her eyes against the sunlight, she swore under her breath as she patted the ground, feeling for her phone.

'Geez, I don't even have a mirror,' she muttered as Millie and Oliver slowly pushed themselves upright, still fuzzy-headed.

'I was just telling these, um, young ladies, we'll be on our way soon,' Archie said, alerting them to the visitors.

Jemima rolled onto her knees, cottoning on to Archie's strategy, and played along.

'Oh yes,' she said, not yet properly seeing the visitors. 'We'll be going soon.' 'Oh, there's no hurry.' The woman was fascinated by

Jemima's peculiar appearance and strange accent. *It's a female wearing short trousers*, she thought. *Ee, I've never seen anythin' like it. Showing her legs like that.* She was intrigued by the foreigners and didn't want them gone yet.

'I'm Ann ... Ann Harmsworth,' she said with a slight bob of her head.

Jemima moved nearer wearing a forced smile. Conscious of their quizzical gazes, she was glad she'd turned her t-shirt inside out.

'Nice to meet you,' Jemima said in a clipped manner. 'But we really must go now.'

Following her cue, Millie and Oliver got to their feet but saw that the three seated figures were blocking their way. Jemima tried to curb her agitation as the trio kept gaping at her. *Keep calm*, she told herself but her mind was racing. *Are they deliberately cornering us?*

'If you're lost, we may be of service,' Ann said. 'Been here over three years now, you know.'

Ignoring Jemima's 'No, No,' she continued. 'Me dear pa ... He was a marine but he died soon as we landed here. And me little brother Tom, he died too.' The words spilled from her, as if she'd waited years to tell someone.

'Oh ...' Jemima began, but Ann blurted on.

'And me ma, she's gettin' married again soon and then we're settling on Norfolk Island. But Mary here,' she pointed to her companion. 'Her ma's a convict. Got life, she did. But Mary, she's me friend. Ay, Mary, we ain't been called ladies before, have we?'

Mary responded with a wide smile, displaying broken front teeth. 'Mary Mullins, at your service,' she said in a lilting voice, dipping her head and fidgeting with the hem of her frayed skirt.

It was now clear to Archie that they were both much younger than he'd originally thought. They wore floppy cotton caps but their sunburnt faces, chafed lips and rough hands told of hard outdoor work. *They're probably in their mid-teens*, he thought, possibly

58

younger than himself. He noticed Mary also had long crimson welts up her arms.

The little boy was vying for attention now, opening and closing his mouth to make popping sounds. Archie leaned towards the lad, whom he imagined to be about six.

'And what's your name?' he asked.

'I'm Henry Kable junior, but everyone calls me young Harry,' he said, pushing his chin out and thumbing his chest. 'Me da, who's Henry Kable senior, he's a consta ... constab ...' he stuttered, then turned to Ann. 'What's me da called again?'

'He's trying to say his pa's a constable,' Ann said. 'But he's really just a convict who's managed to get in good with the gov'nor. It's a long story, see ...' At the mention of *constable*, she'd seen the foreigners bristle. She didn't want them to leave yet.

'We *really* must get going now. Come on guys, let's get moving,' Archie said, at the same time scanning the escarpment for the best route down through the forest.

Oliver, who'd been leaning against the rock wall, now limped forwards, groaning with the effort. The visitors, noticing his swollen ankle for the first time, shuffled aside to let him through.

'Maybe we should try getting some food first,' Oliver said, not seeing Archie glaring at him to shut him up. 'I'm starving!'

'Sprained ankle?' said Mary, looking Oliver up and down. 'You mustn't be putting weight on that. Just along there's a berry bush ... a bit sour like but ...' She turned to Archie. 'That's where we was headed when we saw youse. We can show youse, but then we got to deliver young Harry to school.'

'I meant *proper* food,' said Oliver, pulling a face at the thought of sour berries. 'We've hardly had a thing since we left home.'

'It's true then, what we've heard? There's a place o' plenty yonder in them mountains?'

'Mm,' Archie said, having no idea what she was talking about. They had to get away before anyone else arrived. They didn't want to be hauled before a military committee, facing questions they couldn't answer.

'Don't worry,' said Ann, seeing the tension. 'We'll not tell a soul we've seen youse.' Turning to her friend, she said, 'Mary Mullins here won't say nothing, will you, Mary?'

'I won't breathe a word,' Mary replied in a solemn tone, and Jemima sensed they were genuine.

'And I won't breathe a word, neither,' said young Harry with a serious expression.

Then, returning to the subject of food, Ann said, 'There ain't much food in the stores, and the ration's to be reduced again soon, so they say. But I s'pose I could spare a wee bit o' pork, seein' as you're ...' She paused, looking from one to the other. 'But you'll 'ave to come with us,' she said, pointing to the ridge. 'Cos we're late now ... and we'll be in trouble cos we've still got jobs to do.'

'I can give youse a wee bit o' bread,' said Mary. 'We're just over yonder. Me hut's at the end of the row, and Ma's out working.'

'No we can't, but thank you. We must get away ASAP - I mean, as soon as possible.'

'Oh, don't fret. There's no-one about. They're all working ... or at the wharf loading the ship for Captain Hunter's sailing. Some marines are leavin' for the old country too, so everythin's abuzz between the barracks and t'other side of the cove.'

'Aye, she's right. There'll be no-one hereabouts,' Mary agreed, with a vigorous nod of her chin. 'They're all t'other side of the cove,' she repeated. 'Dead as a doornail 'round our huts.'

'We can't take that risk, ladies,' said Archie, shaking his head.

'Actually, Archie, if it's such a short distance, and there's no-one around maybe we *should* take the risk to get food, seeing Ann and Mary are kind enough to offer,' said Jemima. And as if it was unanimously decided, Jemima turned to Oliver, telling him he'd have to stay put. He was about to object, so she leaned closer to him.

'Ollie, if we need to make a quick getaway, you'll slow us down. We won't be long.' When Millie began to protest, she whispered,

'We need you with us, Mil – just in case.' She added a furtive wink that Millie didn't understand. Turning to the others, she said, 'Come on, then. Let's go.'

'We'll 'ave to skip our berry-picking – young Harry needs to get to school or they'll be sending a search party.' Anne took a couple of steps away and spoke to Mary in a low voice. Mary nodded.

Millie turned to Oliver, slouched against the rock wall, and laid the water canteen beside him.

'We won't be long.'

He gave a sullen nod, crossing his arms against his chest as Millie disappeared around the escarpment with the others.

****

Chapter 11

Separation

Ann led the way up the slope with young Harry prancing beside her. The others followed two abreast unless manoeuvring between bushes and boulders. Millie walked with Mary.

'You don't even know our names … I'm Millie.'

Mary nodded and smiled but that was all.

'You said your name's Mary Mullins. Is that Irish?'

'Aye, Ma's from Ireland.'

'It's just that something about your name rings a bell.'

'Rings a bell? What's that? Ee, you lot talk funny.'

'It means I've heard it before … somewhere.'

'Me ma's Hannah Mullins,' Mary said. 'Lucky she was spared the noose; got sent here instead.'

Millie felt goosebumps up her arms. She had vague memories of her mum saying she had an Irish ancestor of 'convict stock' with the name Mullins, from way back. She wanted to ask more but knew she couldn't explain any of it to Mary; it was all too bizarre. As they approached the ridge, she felt an uneasiness stewing in her gut, recalling the last time they'd peered over the crest.

Pelicans soared above like silver origami birds against an aqua-blue sky. Ann paused at the hilltop where, concealed behind bushes, they could see across to the opposite shore around the timber wharf. As she'd predicted, there was much coming and going. Men were carrying boxes and rolling barrels along the wharf to be loaded onto the lonely ship in the cove. The area between there and the governor's house was a hive of activity.

Ann signalled for them to sit. 'Now, the plan is I'll go ahead and deliver young Harry to school. Mary will take you to her hut; it's closer than mine. I live nearer the barracks and there's always something goin' on there.' She paused and they heard commands wafting from the direction they'd already imagined was the military camp. 'I'll meet you there with the pork. Come on lad; we're already late,' she said as she and Harry rose to leave.

Jemima leaned close to the boy. 'Remember, not a word. Our secret,' she said, finger to her lip.

He pressed his mouth into a crooked smile and gave a silent nod.

'Say farewell, then,' Ann said to the boy, but he was already running ahead.

'I hope he doesn't blab ... I mean, talk about us,' said Archie to Mary.

'Well, if he does, no-one will pay attention. He's just a wee lad who loves tellin' tales ... Our hut's just down along here.' She led the way down the slope.

'Mary?' Archie asked, looking towards the water. 'Yesterday we saw some Kooris getting out of their canoes down there ...'

'Kooris?'

'I mean natives. One of them was injured, bleeding pretty bad. Do you know what happened?'

'No, but they was likely digging up tatties – potatoes, I mean – from a patch along the way. The guards are meant to just scare 'em off, but they've been known to put a bullet in one or two ... But really, they ask for it, taking what's not theirs.'

As Mary walked ahead, Archie glared at the back of her head. *What!* he mouthed.

'Aye, it looks like there's something ado down there too ... at the hospital,' Mary said over her shoulder, pointing to a huddle of ramshackle structures by the water's edge. They could hear faint voices.

'The hospital?' said Jemima in disbelief as she looked towards a jumble of canvas tents clustered around a crudely built central building.

'Aye, but they've started a new one.' Mary nodded in the

direction of the building site, where yesterday they'd seen convicts dragging a cart. As she spoke, a group of soldiers appeared outside the hospital building and began heading back along the track to the main settlement. They were deep in animated conversation

'I thought you said there'd be no-one around,' said Jemima, turning on Mary with a scowl.

'Well, there must've been an accident,' Mary replied, her brow creased. 'They're going now, anyway, so we'll head that way, then along a path to our hut. They'll be well gone by the time we get there.'

As they reached the edge of the hospital precinct and crouched behind a stand of bushes, they heard loud groans coming from the main building. The cries became increasingly louder and more desperate before a male voice began screaming.

'No, please no!' the voice blared. The words were repeated, over and over, becoming more frantic. Then, all went quiet.

'I'm going to have a peek,' Mary said abruptly. 'I'll be hidden by the woodheap. I'll call you over if it's safe.'

Before they could object, she left them. They had no choice but to watch as she darted across the clearing, stopping next to the main building, where they saw her face pressed against the slab wall, her hands cupped around her cheeks, peering through a crack. She was partially concealed by a huge pile of firewood.

'We don't have time for this!' Jemima snarled, looking to her right and left. 'If I'd known this was going to happen … Look, she's signalling for us to go over there. We'd better had … quick.'

When they reached her crouched against the wall, her flushed expression told them she thought it was worth the risk. She was clearly unable to contain her excitement.

Shush, she mimed at them, before whispering breathlessly, 'I just heard the surgeon telling his offsider some soldiers were doin' practice when one accidently shot t'other … up here.' She pointed towards her thigh. 'I heard him say, *"The poor lad's got to lose his leg … it has to come off!"* That's what he said! Have a look!' She stabbed her finger at the viewing hole. 'I heard the surgeon say "*amputation*"! Go on, have a look!'

Archie and Millie's eyes stretched in horror, but Jemima was overtaken with a ghoulish curiosity she couldn't resist. She didn't wait for uncertainty to set in before putting her eye to the crack.

A scrawny white body lay unconscious on a wooden operating table, its arms hanging over the sides. The young man, his head lolling to the side, was facing her. *Thank goodness, his eyes are shut,* she thought, seeing the deeply sunken hollows. She could see deathly - white legs and feet protruding beyond the surgeon's bent body. She felt both relief and disappointment that the doctor was blocking her view of the area to be dealt with. Next to the table, a metal container on the floor was catching a steady trickle of blood.

'It's a last resort!' she heard one of the men say in earnest to the other. 'He won't live if I don't take it off, man! Do you think for one minute I want to?' The last words were a high-pitched appeal. Jemima could hear the distress in the surgeon's voice. She felt her throat constrict in pity for the young life lying there.

There was a short pause before a voice said, 'At least he's out to it now. We'd better make a start before he comes to again. We'll need laudanum on hand.'

The other man nodded and reached for a bottle of reddish-brown liquid. He grabbed a type of handsaw and passed it to the surgeon.

'We'll need men to hold him down when he comes round.'

Jemima looked away and sat back on her haunches, feeling pale and exhausted. Mary leaned in for another look. *There's no way I'll look again,* thought Jemima. Millie and Archie were staring at her.

'What did you see, Jem?'

'I don't want to talk about it,' she snapped. 'I just want to get out of here,' she said to Mary as she straightened up, trying to control the emotion raging in her chest. *Is this grief or rage?*

'Our hut's just along here,' said Mary quietly, with obvious disappointment. It wasn't the response she'd expected. 'We don't have to pass any more buildings – we're on the end of a row.'

They walked on in silence till Archie said to his sister, 'You didn't have to look.'

Jemima bit down on her lip. He was right. Behind them, the screams started up again. Jemima put her hands over her ears and quickened her pace. *Why did I look?*

'I didn't actually *see* anything,' she said to Archie as he caught up with her. 'It's just this place. It's like being in a nightmare.'

'We'll be out of here soon,' said Millie, squeezing her cousin's hand. 'Soon as we can ...'

****

Chapter 12

Mary Mullins

'Here we are,' said Mary, turning towards a coarsely built hut with a small higgledy-piggledy patch of garden in front. The roof was covered with cabbage tree palm fronds above timber-slatted walls partly covered with caked mud. One end had a stone chimney attached. The window spaces had no glass – only timber rods crisscrossed the opening. To one side of the dirt path a sad pumpkin vine rambled between other plants wilting in the dry, sandy ground.

'The drought's been terrible bad,' Mary said, seeing them eye it. 'It's been so hot we've had birds and bats falling out of the sky and landing at our feet.'

Jemima cast a disbelieving glance at Millie, who surprised her by mouthing that it was true.

'I read about it,' she whispered. '... an El Niño weather cycle in the early 1790s.'

Mary pushed the door open with difficulty. 'There ain't enough hinges to go round, see,' she explained over her shoulder. 'So we had to use rope.'

Jemima followed her through the entry and was shocked by the crudeness that confronted her. Inside was stale smelling, reeking of urine, wood smoke and old fat. She tried not to gag. The floor was made of packed earth, dark-stained in places. Sunlight was visible through cracks in the walls and a stone fireplace dominated one end of the room with orange coals still twinkling in the soot.

'Ee, I'd better get the fire stoked,' said Mary, dropping her to knees to feed small split logs onto it. 'I've not done any of me jobs here yet ...'

They stood in dazed silence near the doorway, taking in the dismal setting and watching as the flames jumped into life. 'Ouch!'

Mary pulled her arm back and spat onto another crimson welt forming on it. Millie wondered what it must be like, cooking in the hut in the heat of summer.

A small table and three stools sat close to the middle of the room. In the far corner, what looked like sacking mattresses were piled in a heap. The horizontal wall frames acted as shelves for tin mugs and bowls. Mary turned from the fire and took a couple of steps to a small cupboard, which consisted of a timber box standing on rickety legs that in turn stood in a tray of murky water, a stained cloth covered the front opening.

'We've had ants again lately, but that stops 'em getting to the food,' Mary explained, seeing her visitors contemplating the timber legs standing in water. She took out a piece of flat bread and broke a portion off with her hand and laid it on the wooden table. 'S'pose Ma'll think we've had rats again too,' she said with a hint of a smile.

'Where do you store your stuff? I mean clothes and sheets and towels?' Jemima asked.

'Well, we're either wearin' it or washin' it, aren't we?' Mary said, pointing through the latticed window to a line strung between bushes with clothes hanging over it. 'What a thing to ask,' she said with a sideward glance.

'But where do you wash and shower?' Millie said, peering around. She felt her cheeks flush as soon as the word *shower* left her lips. *Of course, they wouldn't have indoor showers yet*, she thought.

'I mean, you have a sink or tub, don't you?' she said, unsure of the right word.

'We wash in the stream o' course, or bring a bucket back; it's better 'n before when we had to walk further.' Mary was becoming irritated by the questions and by the way they were staring around the room. 'Look, I have to do me jobs – if you got time for questions, can you give us a hand before you go? I've got me other job then, down in the town.'

She pushed a crude straw broom into Jemima's hand and

pointed towards the leaves that had blown through the doorway. Jemima began flicking at them with a bemused look that said, *Why bother sweeping a dirt floor?*

It was clear from Mary's brusque manner that they'd offended her, but Millie simply couldn't imagine how anyone could live for years without a sink or a wardrobe, or a fridge ... or a hair dryer for that matter. She wanted to ask how she'd survived without a microwave or a toaster, but instead she said, 'What do you want *me* to do, Mary? We can spare a few minutes ...' Mary gave a tight smile and nodded to the far end of the room.

'Well, the chamber pot needs emptying, the mattresses need shaking of vermin, the furniture needs the dirt wiping off it,' she said matter-of-factly. 'I'd say wood needs choppin' and bringing in,' she said, looking at Archie, 'but you'd best not linger outside.'

Millie decided the least loathsome job was wiping the table and stools with a rag that Mary had indicated hanging from a wooden peg. The curiously primitive set-up had distracted them from their mission, as there was no sign of anyone around.

'How do you keep your food cool?' Archie asked, picking up one of the bracken-stuffed mattresses and shaking it where he stood.

'Ee, don't shake it there like that, lad ...' She gave an impatient shake of her head, as falling bugs and cockroaches scurried under the remaining mattresses. 'Just leave it and I'll take 'em outside later. Ee, that's an odd question you're askin' me. I'd say the same way *you* keep *your* food cool. We put wet cloth over it. Of course, in summer it's near impossible to stop fresh meat from rottin', as you'd know ... Or have youse got some other clever way where youse come from?'

They shrugged, and to change the topic Jemima asked if she did these chores every day.

'Ee, o' course; what a question ... and if truth be told, I have a thing about cleaning, cos I can still smell that filthy condemned cell we were in ... me and Ma. I were only a wee tot and we was in there for ages, Ma told me. It was the dirtiest stinking place. So I'm always cleaning everything now, see.'

'What do you mean, *condemned* cell?'

'It's where they put Ma in Newgate Prison, awaiting the noose … They said she was a *forger* see – said she faked someone's will – you know, when someone leaves you stuff after they die. But it were true – a sailor give her a letter saying she could get wages owed him if he died.' Mary's voice was unsteady. 'But they didn't believe her, see. Anyway, she got sent here, instead of the noose.'

'Oh …' was all Jemima could manage. She felt bad now for sneering at sweeping a dirt floor.

'She's married to Mr Peat now … He got life an' all for highway robbery, but they've found their place now. He's overseer to the timber cutters and I've a wee sister and Ma's havin' another … She don't really need me looking out for her no more. It's me that needs …'

'Mary, we *really* need to get going now …' Jemima said as kindly as she could.

'Oh aye, o' course,' said Mary, taking the bread from the table and wrapping it in an old cloth. 'Ee, I wonder why Ann's not here with the pork?'

Suddenly panicked, Jemima turned to Millie and Archie. 'We have to get the hell out of here in case young Harry couldn't keep his mouth shut.'

Mary was about to say something in defence of Harry when a shadow filled the room.

'What's this, then?' A tall, heavy-set man with a deep voice spoke from the doorway. Jemima felt the hair on her neck stand on end.

'This is me new da, Mr Peat,' said Mary quickly.

Jemima quickly got a grip and said, 'Sir, we've lost our way and, er, Mary here is kindly giving us a little bread to help us on our way.' Jemima wished she'd taken out the piercings and left her head unshaved.

Mary Mullins

'Well, that's all well an' good, but I don't think that's possible. The soldiers are on their way.'

****

Chapter 13

Mr Peat

'Soldiers … on the way?' Jemima gasped, feeling the breath being sucked from her lungs.

'Aye, rounding people up, they are. Assemblin' them to watch the flogging,' Mr Peat said as he took in the strangers' appearance and their obvious fear at his presence.

'What flogging?' said Mary in utter surprise. No sooner had her question erupted than a soldier's voice was heard behind Mr Peat's hefty frame.

'Anyone not working away from the settlement is required to assemble for the flogging along by the barracks,' the voice boomed.

Mr Peat turned his huge bulk, blocking the soldier's view, and said, 'I'll see to it, sir. I'll make sure those here attend.'

They heard the soldier mutter something and he was gone.

'Thank you, sir; we'll be off now,' said Jemima, head down and making for the doorway with the others following.

'Er, not so fast,' said Mr Peat, blocking their exit. 'It's clear you're not from round here, by the look 'n sound of youse, but …'

'They've just lost their way,' Mary interrupted, trying to aid their departure.

Jemima gave a silent but energetic nod. *The less I open my mouth the better*, she thought.

Mr Peat, knowing there was no time for an account, resisted asking *From where?*

He'd also heard talk of a place beyond the Blue Mountains, a place where no-one was obliged to work, but he'd thought it nonsense. Now, looking at these youngsters, he didn't know what to think. He was curious to know what the taller one had done to warrant having her head shaved in such a way, not to mention the strange garb they all wore. But he decided they looked harmless enough, from his experience of criminal character.

'With a past like mine, I'll not involve meself.' He spoke as if deep in thought, recalling his own history of escape and capture. Then, turning to Mary, he said, 'But they can't just bolt out the door and head in t'other direction. That'll raise the alarm and we'll all be drawn in.' To the strangers, he said, 'I'm surprised you got this far, looking like that ... but o' course you can't stay ...'

'Here, lad, put this on,' he said, handing Archie his tattered hat and a jacket from behind the door. Archie eyed the stained collar, dark with caked-on sweat, but shuffled into it without a word. It hung like an overcoat on his frame.

'I'll get our petticoats and shifts off the line, then,' said Mary as she headed outside.

As she passed him, Mr Peat whispered, 'The shaved one'll need Ma's straw hat.' Then turning to the others, he said, 'When you get outside, fall in at back of yon crowd headin' to the flogging. Keep your heads down and keep walking. You'd best get them things off if you're to blend in,' he said, pointing to their shoes. 'I'll not be involved, so the lass will lead youse.'

Mary returned and handed out the coarse garments, telling the girls it was lucky the women had just been issued new slops. They pulled them over their clothes, the petticoats acting as long skirts. Meanwhile Mr Peat stood in the doorway, looking right and left.

'Why don't we just wait here till everyone's gone to watch the flogging, and then we slip away?' Jemima suggested in desperation, as he went to step forwards.

'No, no ... they're doin' the rounds now, herding the stragglers and checking who's missing. There may not be many about the huts here but take a wrong turn and you'll be seized by a guard. No, no; timing's everything when it comes to gettin' away.'

Jemima opened her mouth again but was cut off before her protest erupted.

'There'll be a bunch o' them natives there today, so that could be just the diversion youse need,' he said addressing them collectively.

'Oh aye, I remember what this flogging's about now,' Mary said, nodding to herself. 'It's about that convict caught stealing fishing tackle belonging to them native women.' Then, turning to Jemima, standing beside her, she said, 'Cos that's forbidden by the gov'nor, see. So he's ordered a floggin' as an example … wants to show them natives how to be civilised, like.'

'Enough talk … Time to move,' said Mr Peat, frowning at Mary. Then, turning to the strangers, he said, 'Like I told youse, keep your 'eads down and keep walking towards the barracks with Mary. When the time's right, she'll show youse how to slip away.'

Seeing there was no point arguing, they nodded. Mr Peat stepped out the door and was gone.

Oh yeah, right; just like that … What the hell have I got us into? We could've done without bread, Jemima thought to herself. Her nerves were jangled; never had she felt so afraid of treading through a doorway. The smelly, repulsive little hut had suddenly become a haven.

****

Chapter 14

The Flogging

Hearts thumping, hardly breathing, they followed Mary along a pathway between crude dwellings, keeping their eyes to the ground. As predicted, there was no-one near the huts but ahead of them, in the direction of the barracks, a motley crowd dawdled towards a distant rhythmic beating of drums. They fell in to the rear of the group, relieved that no-one looked back. Jemima saw they were barefooted and wore little more than rags. The smell of stale bodies was inescapable. From the way they moved, she imagined their expressions would be insipid, their eyes reflecting the depressing condition of their lives. From further ahead, the shrieks of small children now mingled with the drumbeat and the hum of a crowd.

'This is ridiculous,' Jemima murmured under her breath. 'We shouldn't be here.'

'Shush.'

They were passing more rows of huts, still heading in the general direction of the barracks when, out of the blue, Mary mumbled, 'This way then,' and pointed to a side path crisscrossed with tree roots.

Ducking off the track, but still bearing towards the noisy assembly, she turned along another path and headed behind what appeared to be a storehouse higher up the hill. Then she veered to the right again, heading further up and across the slope. She stopped behind a large rock protruding from the hillside above the uppermost row of huts and checked behind as the others caught up, putting her hand up to make sure no-one spoke. Then, skirting an area strewn with felled timber and deserted sawpits, she led the way to a further outcrop hemmed by low bushes.

'That was risky, sorry,' she whispered at last. 'But no-one took no notice.' She dropped to her haunches and they collapsed beside her in nervous exhaustion. They were overlooking a clearing, with a view of open space between the end of the convict men's huts and the barracks.

'It's a military parade ground,' Archie said in a voice barely audible. A crowd of almost a hundred was already milling around the edge of the barren, dusty area with tree stumps littering its margins.

As they caught their breath, they saw a huddle of convict men, some in leg irons, shuffling from the opposite direction. One of their guards was bullying them along, bawling, 'C'mon. We 'aven't got all day.' Some were chained together; two had heavy-looking iron collars around their necks, thick spikes jutting from either side, so that they could barely turn their heads.

'How can they work like that?' Archie said under his breath, shaking his head in disbelief.

'They brought it on themselves, stealin' food from others' gardens,' said Mary. 'Don't deserve an ounce of pity, if you ask me.'

Archie didn't reply; he felt anger tightening his gut at such cruelty. He could already relate to the hungry bellies of those men. The risk they'd taken for a bit of bread and dried pork – a futile risk as it turned out – made him want to yell at Jemima for getting them into this mess. But, seeing her pale, tense face, he tried to swallow his agitation.

'So what's going to happen?' asked Millie, scanning anxious eyes over the assembly below.

'Aye, don't tell me you've not seen a floggin' afore?' Mary looked from one to the other, stunned when they shook their heads. 'How's that possible? How do they keep youse all in line then – where youse come from?' When no-one offered a response, she said, 'S'pose you'll just have to see for yourselves, then.'

'Are we safe here, do you think, Mary?' Millie asked, looking behind them.

'Aye, I'd say so. They're all taken with the doings now,' said

Mary, inspecting the crowd. Then, following Millie's gaze across the rear ridge, she said mysteriously, 'Only the wilds to fear that way.'

What did she mean by that? Millie wanted to ask but it seemed the event was about to begin.

A triangular frame stood at the centre of the clearing. As a command was bellowed, the crowd opened to allow a chained convict, bare from the waist up, to be jostled forwards by two soldiers. He was hustled to the structure and tied to it so that his arms were above his head. The crowd hushed.

Jemima pointed to a large number of Aboriginal men and women who had also been ushered to the front of the gathering, closest to the flogging frame. She exchanged a puzzled look with Archie. 'Why ...?'

Anticipating her question, Mary said, 'Oh, they're always in town now; staying at the gov'nor's house, some of 'em ... or at Bennelong's house over yonder,' she said, nodding across the cove. 'Had a brick house built for him, the gov'nor did ...' Seeing their reaction to Bennelong's name, she continued.

'Seems you've heard o' him, then? He's right favoured by the gov'nor and officers – hand and glove they are now. There was trouble before, though – the gov'nor even got speared by one of 'em, but he bore it so's to make peace, it's said. Come and go as they please now, they do.'

'But ...'

Mary ignored the interruption and continued with a giggle, 'Ee, I didn't know where to look when they first come into town, cos they didn't bother coverin' up, you know.' She blushed with the memory.

'But why are they here for the ...?'

'Cos it's on *their* behalf, see; like I said before ... the gov'nor wants 'em to watch the flogging so's they understand proper justice, see ... I expect they'll explain it to 'em just now.'

She looked back at the scene as a voice boomed out from below. A straight-backed man addressed the assorted gathering:

'The gov'nor has ordered that this thief be severely flogged in the presence of those assembled who were robbed of their fishing tackle,' he paused and gestured specifically at two Aboriginal women at the front of the crowd.

'What's he mean by *severely* flogged?' Archie whispered, without taking his gaze off the man's taut body tied against the frame, his back already gleaming with sweat in the morning heat.

'Couple o' hundred lashes maybe,' Mary said matter-of-factly. 'Likely won't get 'em all at once, cos it'd stop him working.'

Archie shuddered, his eyes still on the convict.

Another man now came forwards holding a whip made of several thick leather strands, each strand having knots along its end.

'Cat-o'-nine-tails,' whispered Millie. 'They look edgy now, those women.'

As the flogger positioned himself, behind the convict, no-one in the crowd moved or spoke. Then, lifting his muscled arm to its full height, he paused as if taking aim; then brought the lash down with all his strength against the man's flesh with a loud crack. The convict's back arched and his head flipped back with the impact of the blow but he didn't utter a sound, though a murmur trickled through the crowd.

Millie put her hand to her mouth but could not look away as crimson welts appeared across the man's shoulder blades.

The flogger lifted his arm again, paused as he shuffled his feet to get a better position, and again brought the whip down with full force into the man's upper body. This time the leather knots tore into his skin as they crisscrossed and bit into his naked back.

Millie looked across to her cousins and met their wide-eyed stares.

Mary watched them with intense interest. *How could they've never seen a floggin' before?*

'You'll be seeing his backbone by fifty lashes,' she said, feeling a mischievous pleasure at their cringes.

Millie put her hands over her ears to block out the whacking sound of each blow. At the front of the crowd one of the native women also had her hands to her face and appeared to be troubled.

Next to her, a taller woman had her hands on her hips, showing strong disapproval of the method of punishment. Then she began shaking a fist and shouting something at the flogger. But the whipping continued, lash after lash. With each blow the man's back became more sliced and bloodied.

'They're savages!' Archie spat in outrage as Millie began quietly sobbing. Jemima had sat pale and silent since the flogging began. Now she dropped her head into her hands.

'Ee, you're right there,' Mary nodded in response to Archie. 'But the gov'nor's trying to civilise 'em, see ... Now that they're living amongst us ... he's showing 'em how to act proper and ...'

'I mean the *British* ... *they're* the savages ...' Archie snapped; his voice broke so that he couldn't continue. Below, the steady slapping of leather against mashed flesh continued.

'Can't you see it's *wrong* ... what they're doing ...' he broke off, aware that he was taking out his repulsion of the blood-spattered scene on Mary. He took a gulp of air, trying to control his emotion.

Mary looked back at him blankly. She opened her mouth to speak as a murmur went through the crowd below, drawing their attention back to the flogging.

The taller Aboriginal woman had picked up a stick, and was attacking the flogger with it. The crowd had erupted into a low rumble as they watched in disbelief. The flogging had ceased.

'I have to go an' show me face ...' Mary flicked Archie a hard stare before addressing the others. 'Stay low till I'm back ... I'll be needing them things back an' all,' she said, eyeing their borrowed clothes. Without a backward glance, she stepped from behind the rock and headed down the slope, veering around the lower side of the storehouse, deliberately passing close by a guard as she neared the crowd.

'It's not *her* fault.' Jemima frowned at her brother. 'What if she dobs us in now? She didn't *have* to help us, you know.'

Archie clenched his jaw and lowered his head but said nothing.

Below, a thunderous voice addressed the crowd again as the prisoner's ropes were cut from the bloodstained frame. His limp body was caught by two men and placed onto an open cart. The official spokesman was telling the crowd they were to immediately resume their duties. The crowd began to disperse in a lethargic trickle.

'C'mon, show's over; get moving. He won't be having the rest of his stripes till he's healed,' a voice roared in an aggressive manner.

Another officer, looking hot and bothered in his fitted red jacket, was standing next to the agitated woman, who was still waving her arms at the motionless body lying on the cart. The officer, by nodding and using reassuring gestures, was trying to console her, but to no avail. The other woman was sitting on the ground, still sobbing.

'Look! *They* can see it's wrong,' Archie said, nodding to them. 'How come all the others just stood there, watching?'

'I recognise them now,' Jemima whispered to herself. 'Those women … they were at Dawes Point yesterday,' she said, turning to Millie and Archie. 'They were the ones laughing with Mr Dawes, remember? When he was writing in his journal?'

'Yeah, and I think that's Bennelong,' said Millie, pointing to an Aboriginal man also wearing a red jacket with silver epaulets. Her own sobbing had eased and, as she wiped her eyes with the back of her hand, she looked behind them up the slope.

Reading her thoughts, Archie said, 'Do you think we should make a dash for it now?'

Millie nodded immediately.

'I think so too,' Jemima said. 'And we can eat once we're in the clear,' she added, revealing the bread under her shift. Seeing their surprise, she gave a weak smile. 'I grabbed it off the table before we left.'

At the mention of food, Millie thought of her brother for the first time in hours.

The Flogging

'Poor Ollie must be starving … and wondering what's happened.'

****

Chapter 15

Oliver

Oliver sat with his back to the rock wall, gazing into the forest that sloped away from him, and cursed his sprained ankle. He didn't like being left behind; he didn't like missing out on the action. He sighed heavily. Out of habit he reached into his pocket for his puffer and again realised it wasn't there. *Haven't needed it*, he thought, *since the tunnel*.

Recalling the tunnel lifted his mood. Maybe he could save the day by finding it before the others got back. It had to be somewhere close. He undid the twine that Nanberry had wrapped around his ankle and pulled aside the paperbark bandage to examine his foot. It was mottled purple and black, but not as swollen. He struggled to his feet using the wall as support as he scanned the forest deciding which way to go, but felt a sharp twinge as he put weight on his foot.

Nope, won't get far on my own, he thought, with another exasperated sigh. He sank against the rock wall again and retied the twine, still pondering the tunnel. At least he could work on his time-travel theory.

Yesterday when he'd mentioned *tesseract* the others hadn't heard of it. *Surprising*, he thought, *seeing the Marvel superhero movies depict a tesseract as a blue cube holding enough power to create a cosmic wormhole*. Anyway, he was far more interested in its real, scientific concept. Now – after turning up here, in another time – he wanted to be an astrophysicist more than ever, to unravel the mystery of time travel.

I'll explain the theory to them with a diagram, he thought, feeling his excitement bubbling. He shuffled closer to the empty fireplace and picked up a short stick. Dragging it through the charcoal, he loaded it with soot and drew a line on the flat weathered rock in front of him.

I'll explain the different dimensions, step by step. He drew more lines to make a square, tracing its height and width, its two dimensions. Then he added more lines to make a cube.

'A cube is a three-dimensional shape,' he'd say, pointing out its height, width *and* depth. He imagined Jemima raising her brows as if to say 'Who doesn't know that?' but he needed to start with the basics. He tried to recall how his science teacher had explained three dimensions with examples:

'We live in a three-dimensional world where we can move left or right, backwards and forwards, and up or down ... But there are *other dimensions* that aren't so easy to imagine.' He'd pause here to let that sink in.

Returning to his cube drawn with charcoal, Oliver tried to add more lines to depict a further dimension, a cube within a cube – what's called a tesseract – but the diagram became a mishmash of smudgy lines. It wasn't going to work.

If only I had the internet, he thought, *there'd be animations of a tesseract. But here, I'll have to try to explain it as a shape*.

'Whatever direction we move in,' he remembered his teacher saying, 'we're also moving through *time*. We can't separate space from time, so we have a concept, or dimension, we call space-time.'

He imagined standing in front of his sister and cousins – but particularly in front of Jemima – pacing like a science lecturer, with her in awe of his knowledge.

'We know other dimensions exist, but they're a mystery, like time itself ...' He'd pause again, before delivering his punch line:

'That is, until now ... cos we *have* entered another dimension, haven't we!' he saw himself announcing the fact, arms outstretched. *It's mind boggling*, he thought, realising he'd also said it aloud.

He imagined Jemima trying to look disinterested but unable to resist asking: 'And what's this got to do with the tunnel?'

'Good question!' he'd say. And for his answer he could rave on about Einstein's theories, or hypothetical 'faster than light' particles – but it'd be too complicated. He had to keep it simple.

'I think the tunnel was a passage through space-time – like a cosmic wormhole, which I'll explain,' he'd say. He imagined Jemima rolling her eyes again. He knew words couldn't really explain what was pretty much unexplainable, so he'd try drawing it again. Turning back to his charcoal diagram, he erased all the lines with his hand.

Maybe I start with how gravity bends space-time, he thought. *But how do I draw a wormhole through space-time? It's such a far-out concept!*

Then it came to him. Looking down at the twine tied around his foot, he saw how he could easily *demonstrate* it. He felt excitement grab at his gut as the pieces started fitting together.

He quickly undid the twine and laid it on the ground in a straight line on the rock in front of him. Then seeing a small, slow-moving beetle, he picked it up and placed it at one end of the twine. Yep, he loved the idea! This is going to *show* how a wormhole is a short cut through space-time.

'Imagine,' he'd say, 'this beetle moving along the twine, heading to the other end. It'd take a certain amount of time to get from one end to the other, like any journey.'

'But – and this is the exciting part – if you bend the twine so that the ends meet, the beetle doesn't have to travel the length of string to get to the other end. Bending the twine creates a short cut.'

In order to demonstrate it, he picked up the string and made a loop so that the ends met, and laid it carefully back on the ground in a teardrop shape, with the beetle still at the starting place – at the pointy end of the loop. 'And there you have it! A short cut,' he'd announce, pointing to the ends of the string touching. 'It explains how *we* could've taken a short cut through time, to arrive back in 1791!'

Up to this point he'd been pleased with his spiel, but now he imagined Jemima, hands on hips, saying, 'As if! That's rubbish, absolute gobbledygook!'

Well, he thought. *Let her come up with a better idea.*

He knew scientists believed gravity bent space-time, and that's how they thought cosmic wormholes were possible, acting as shortcut passages or bridges connecting distant points in space-time … But that didn't explain why they'd arrived here.

He stretched, realising his neck was aching and his belly was growling with hunger. He took a sip of water. The others were taking a very long time to 'duck over the ridge' for bread and pork, and he was starting to feel agitated. He was shuffling himself into a more comfortable position when he felt, rather than heard, a deep thud to the side of the rock-shelter. He twisted around to see Nanberry had landed with a thump from the rocks above. Oliver saw his shocked, troubled expression at seeing him sitting there.

'Why are you still here, Oliver?' Nanberry said, with a concerned glance across the escarpment. 'Someone will find you here … Where are your friends?' He scanned the forest again. Seeing Oliver hesitate, he gestured for him to get up. 'Quickly, you must move now … to another place … Come!'

Oliver struggled to his feet and followed Nanberry, suddenly fearful for his safety. He wanted to ask Nanberry to slow down, and he wanted to ask why the others could possibly have taken so long, but he was too puffed to talk. They scrambled down the slope with Oliver tripping and falling several times before they eventually stopped to catch their breath near the water's edge. Oliver was gasping; his foot was throbbing.

'Where are your friends?' Nanberry repeated in an impatient manner.

Oliver didn't want to admit they'd overslept, making it impossible to get away before sunrise, so he said, 'They went to find food … over the ridge.'

Nanberry shook his head but said nothing. Then, taking in the exhaustion on Oliver's face and seeing his limp, he said, 'Come, we will go by *nawi* from here.'

Oliver wondered what *nawi* meant, but saw Nanberry heading over to several canoes pulled up onto the sand, partially concealed behind bushes.

'You can rest your foot while I paddle,' said Nanberry, making for the closest vessel.

Oliver felt a rush of panic; he couldn't leave not knowing where the others were, and what had happened to them. But he knew he couldn't stay either.

'Where could they be all this time? I mean, it's been hours!' he said, still standing in the same spot.

Nanberry looked concerned as he walked back a few paces to stand beside Oliver. 'Today a big flogging happened at the barracks.' His expression was sombre. 'Maybe they ...'

'What! Maybe what?' Oliver almost wailed the words.

'Maybe they were ... detained.'

'Detained? You mean caught?'

'I am sorry, but I think they are not good at hiding,' Nanberry said, with a sideward look that said *just as you are not*. Then, glancing up the slope, he continued, 'Today, many people were ordered to watch the flogging. That was good fortune for you ...'

He left his meaning unspoken, but Oliver got the drift. His mind raced with disturbing images before Nanberry's voice cut through his chaotic thoughts.

'But now you cannot stay here.'

'Yes,' Oliver said slowly, feeling his energy drained. 'You are right. I can only find them if I am free.' He hobbled to the water's edge with a stoic, determined expression, thankful for Nanberry's help.

****

Chapter 16

Boorong and Patye

Nanberry waded into the water and eased the nawi part way off the bank. At Nanberry's bidding, Oliver, feeling a nervous flutter, twisted himself into it. He'd never seen such a vessel before, never mind sat in one. Questions flooded his mind and tumbled out one after another.

'Whose canoe, … yours? How come it's made of *bark*? You sure it'll hold us both? How come it's had a fire in it? Is it waterproof? And …' His rush of words stalled when he saw Nanberry bent forwards, his shoulders bouncing with laughter.

'You are funny,' Nanberry spluttered as he pushed off from the sand. He climbed in behind Oliver and paddled into the current before addressing Oliver's questions. 'This is my friend's nawi. He knows I will return it later.' He watched as Oliver ran his hand over the smooth interior of the vessel and examined how at each end the pleats of bark were tied firmly with thick twine.

'Wow, it's made from one piece of bark,' Oliver said in awe.

Nanberry saw the flash of admiration and continued.

'We make our nawi from *goomon*, a tree I will show you.' Oliver nodded, still inspecting the vessel. 'There are many steps to make a good nawi.' Nanberry saw Oliver studying the thick, flattened wad of clay positioned near the front of the nawi. 'That's where we keep a fire to cook our fish.'

'Wow,' Oliver said again, and Nanberry broke into another fit of laughter seeing Oliver speechless with astonishment.

'Before I walked I was in nawis,' Nanberry said between chuckles. 'Every day I was with my mother fishing – all the women singing together.' He stared into the distance now, reliving childhood memories.

As they cut through the water, a flock of ducks lifted from its surface with a noisy, flapping commotion. Oliver sat rigid, careful not to tilt his body for fear of capsizing the vessel, his hands clutching each side as if to balance it. The nawi felt sturdy but he was not a confident swimmer.

Nanberry distracted him, saying, 'You need food, I think. I will show you an easy way to get fish.'

'Gee, thanks, mate,' Oliver said with gusto.

The water shimmered with flecks of silver in the early afternoon sunlight, with only the slightest breeze brushing its surface. The nawi glided smoothly though the water parallel to the bank and Oliver felt his shoulders gradually soften as he breathed in the tranquillity. Despite his anxiety for his sister and the others, he was enjoying this unique experience.

Noticing they'd paddled westwards and around a broad headland, Oliver tried to estimate their whereabouts and decided they were heading into Darling Harbour. The hillside to his left was strewn with rocky outcrops between stands of tall gumtrees. Flowering bushes and tree ferns filled the understorey with a lacy cascade of greens and, closer to shore, she-oaks bent towards the water's edge, a thick layer of pine needles forming a carpet beneath them.

That must be Barangaroo Reserve, he thought. 'Don't suppose you know of any tunnels up that way, do you?' Oliver asked over his shoulder, pointing back over to the slope. 'I think that's where we got lost.'

'Tunnels?'

'Yeah, like a long cave going into the hillside?'

'We have many caves. I will show you tomorrow.'

'Tomorrow? But -'

He was cut short by the sound of indistinct voices coming from beyond the bend ahead. He squinted into the distance to see a group of nawis approaching. As they came closer he saw their paddles lifting and falling in time with a chorus of female voices.

Then it seemed that, on the women spotting him, their melody faded, and the vessels veered into another cove and out of sight – except for one with two occupants, which crossed the water and disappeared behind a huge rock some distance ahead.

'That is Boorong and Patyegarang. You will see them soon,' Nanberry said matter-of-factly. Not waiting for a response, he pointed to a swarm of bees circling a tree trunk near the bank. 'I will get honey later – and maybe eggs,' he added, waving a paddle to where he knew there was a nest, hidden behind reeds.

Oliver nodded, thinking, *This doesn't happen to me every day.*

As Nanberry steered them past the rock formation, Oliver heard female voices again. Gliding closer to shore, he saw two young native women sitting near a small fire; both wore loose-fitting frocks. They looked as if they were expecting Nanberry. He raised his hand and called a greeting, and they responded in the same way. He paddled towards a narrow beach beyond the rock where he jumped out and pulled the nawi ashore. Oliver clambered out and followed Nanberry to the fireside.

'This is Oliver – he is still lost,' Nanberry said as he approached them. 'And this is Boorong and Patyegarang,' he added, nodding to each. They smiled and dipped their heads.

So Nanberry has told them about meeting us, Oliver thought as he bobbed his head in return.

One of them signalled with an outstretched arm for Oliver to sit and, after he'd lowered himself carefully and cradled his swollen ankle, she pulled a bark parcel from the coals, and peeled it open to release a sweet, smoky, mouth-watering aroma. She gestured to what looked like roast potato portions.

'*Midyini* – yam,' she said as Oliver bit into one. And when his throat made deep purring sounds of enjoyment, they all began laughing. As they sat eating, Oliver decided the girls were mid-to-late teens.

'Do you live in Sydney, like Nanberry?' he asked carefully, hoping they understood. He was conscious of their intense gazes and that he'd already forgotten their names.

'No, not me,' the girl beside him said. 'And you can say *Pat-ye* for my name.'

'Pat-ye,' Oliver repeated. 'So why, I mean ...' He hesitated, not knowing how to put his question.

'I visit Mr Dawes often,' Patye said into the silence. 'I teach him language – and he writes words in his book. And he explains English to me. You know Mr Dawes's house at Tar-Ra.'

Oliver nodded, hearing her words as a statement. *So they know we were at Tar-Ra yesterday.*

'Yes,' he said simply, because now more questions were rushing through his mind.

'But I lived in Sydney before,' said the other girl, Boorong. 'I was very sick and they made me well.'

'Sick with smallpox?' Oliver asked, noticing she had pockmarks on her face.

'Yes, then Mrs Johnson nursed me. And taught me English and reading. Then I was go-between for my people and the British. I helped bring friendship between them.'

'Me too,' Nanberry said, thumbing his chest.

'But by and by,' Boorong continued, 'I told Mrs Johnson I want to live with my people again. Now when I visit Sydney, I um ... wear this.' She touched her frock and Oliver realised she'd thought his unspoken question was about their clothes, rather than their English skills. 'We wear this when we meet white people ... because of the custom.'

Oliver nodded and silence settled on their gathering again. Except for the sounds of birds and insects, and the lapping of water, it was quiet and calm.

Nanberry rose and went to a tree, where he peeled strips of paperbark from its trunk. After placing them beside Oliver, he crossed to a small pool in the rock shelf.

'Look, Oliver.'

He knelt, pointing into the water. When Oliver reached him, he saw several good-sized fish moving slowly back and forth in the pool. Nanberry put his hands in and scooped one out so that it lay flapping on the rock.

'How'd you do that so easy?' Oliver blinked open-mouthed from the fish to Nanberry.

'When the tide is low, we put this in the water.' Nanberry picked up some crinkled leaves lying beside the pool and rubbed them between his fingers. 'British people call this *wattle* – these leaves make fish sleepy so it's easy to catch them. Will you eat some more now?'

'You bet,' Oliver replied with a grin. 'I mean, yes!' he said, joining in their contagious laughter. A short while later they sat by the fire in cordial silence, eating flaky pieces of fish, which Nanberry had cooked in the coals.

'I've never done this before,' said Oliver, knowing he'd always remember the experience. He glanced up to catch Boorong observing him. 'I see why you prefer being here, to ...'

Boorong nodded, understanding his unspoken words. 'Governor says we do well to live in Sydney, and follow British ways, for a better life ... And they *do* have good things: blankets, candles and ... clever tools.' She held an imaginary implement between her hands and angled it skywards.

'Telescope,' Patye supplied the word, 'to see a long way.'

Boorong nodded and Oliver could see she was groping for the words to express herself, as he had done earlier. 'They have clever things; but they do not *listen* to ...' She waved her hand to indicate their surroundings – the sky, the birds, water, trees – then she let her arm drop to her side, without finishing.

Oliver cleared his throat. He wanted to say something meaningful but all he said was, 'Yes.'

Meeting his gaze again, she continued. 'My family lived along that river.' She indicated westwards. 'A long time before British made their town at Parramatta. But now, many trees are gone, and yams,' she said, touching the earth. 'Before, we had ducks and eels and fish from that river – now my family must move away. They said to me, "Boorong, tell gov'nor we are angry."' She paused to ensure Oliver's attention.

'And what did he do?' Oliver leaned in with genuine curiosity.

'He … he got their meaning. He saw they were not happy that many British settlers moved to Parramatta … but the next day he sent more soldiers to stay there.'

Oliver didn't know what to say. His mind catapulted through time, playing scenes in fast forward from lessons and videos about Aboriginal people driven off their land, kids taken from their families and then forbidden to speak their language. And he remembered after class his friend saying, 'What's that stuff got to do with us?' There'd been no more discussion; they'd just gone off to play handball.

I should've thought more about it, cos it wasn't right, what happened.

Boorong was staring into the flames and he imagined she was waiting for him to speak. But he felt tongue-tied. He couldn't tell her it would get worse – much worse – before it got better. He couldn't say how many people had suffered before a prime minister finally said sorry for the tragedy of it all.

'One day, they *will* listen,' Oliver said quietly, wanting to assure himself of a happy ending.

Again they sat in silence, absorbed in their thoughts until Patye said, 'Mr Dawes, he listens …'

'Yes, he is a good man.' Boorong winked, and Oliver thought there must be a strong friendship between Patye and Mr Dawes. 'I shall go back now,' she said, and Patye rose with her. 'We must prepare for our corroboree.' She saw Oliver's blank expression and explained, 'Before Captain Hunter sails we shall have song and dance for him and other officers … at Bennelong's Point.'

Nanberry came and crouched beside Oliver. 'After we cover your foot, I must go too. I will dine at the gov'nor's table again with Mr White. They are planning another expedition westwards.

Bennelong wants to go too but Barangaroo, his wife, won't let him.' He finished with a short laugh.

Oliver was struck by how easily Nanberry seemed to move from campfire to the governor's table. Boorong and Patye were also choosing which parts of British life they wanted. Oliver was feeling a surge of admiration for the way they could move between cultures, when something struck him about Boorong's earlier words.

'Boorong, you just said, I shall go *back* now. Did you mean to *Sydney*? Did you visit there today?'

'Yes, gov'nor wished it – for us to watch the flogging.'

Oliver's heart raced. 'Did you see strangers, like me, anywhere?' He glanced down at his out-of-place clothes. 'Maybe, um, you saw them detained by guards?' His gut cramped at the thought.

'No, I did not stay – I do not like floggings.'

Oliver looked away to hide his despair. He just hoped his sister and cousins weren't suffering, whatever had happened to them there.

****

Chapter 17

The Stash

'I have … to stop, I can't …' Millie puffed in breathless spurts as they belly-crawled through the undergrowth. They reached a thick patch of bushes and scrambled under them, red-faced and gasping.

'I hope we're far enough … to rest a bit …' Jemima panted, hunkered under the branches.

Archie peered through the foliage. 'But *where* are we?' he huffed. 'Geez, I wish we had water. It's so freakin' hot …'

'And deodorant,' Millie cut in, waving her hand in front of herself.

Still catching her breath, Jemima pulled Mary's bread from her pocket and handed out portions.

'It'd help if you took that smelly jacket off, you dummy,' she said without looking at her brother.

He ignored her, knowing his elbows would end up as scratched and raw as his knees without it.

'About … the clothes …' Millie found it difficult to speak with dry bread sticking to the roof of her mouth, but she managed a gulp and looked down at her ripped, dirt-streaked shift. 'We should've left them, seeing Mary was good enough to lend them.'

'If we'd waited another second, there was no chance we'd get away,' Jemima said with an irritated edge to her voice. 'A guard was already herding men back up to that sawmill. It's a miracle we've made it.'

Millie and Archie exchanged a look but said nothing, knowing it was true. At Jemima's signal they'd darted up the hill away from the parade ground. Then, ever watchful, they'd skulked through the bush in the direction of Dawes Point, staying well up the slope behind the rows of huts. So far, it seemed, no-one had spotted them.

'We can leave the clothes under the rock-shelter when we get back to Ollie,' said Archie, returning to Millie's comment. He was still trying to gauge their whereabouts. Craning his neck, he spotted a row of rooftops further down the hill, which suggested they were still some way from Dawes Point. 'Once we're past the hospital area, I reckon we head over the ridge and we'll find Ollie okay then.'

Hearing a distant yell from the direction of the barracks, Jemima said, 'Come on, let's go.'

Emerging cautiously from their hiding spot, they alternated between crawling and dashing, depending on their cover. Once they'd reached the area above the hospital precinct, they figured they were a safe distance from the main settlement.

As they crouched, out of breath, Archie pointed silently down the slope towards the sandy bank where they'd seen the injured Aboriginal man the day before. Three unkempt-looking white men were huddled behind bushes at the edge of the beach. A fishing boat approached and, as it neared the shore, they waded out and began unloading items onto the bank. Though engrossed in conversation, they kept looking back across the cove and along the shoreline, to the settlement.

'They're taking advantage of the distraction at the barracks too, I reckon.'

Then the men began carrying the objects away from the water's edge. One had a shovel.

'Get down.' Jemima tried to flatten herself more, while keeping an eye on their movements. When the men stopped near a hollow that was concealed by foliage, she blew a long breath of relief.

Moving between the boat and their hiding spot, the men worked in silence, with one keeping watch. When they'd finished, the words 'on the morrow ... there be no moon', drifted up the slope.

The men were turning to leave when Millie, seeing a spider crawling up her leg, let out an instinctive shriek. The men immediately tensed and spun around to glare towards the escarpment.

'After 'em! They've seen the stash!' one of them growled.

'Run,' Jemima yelled. 'Quick, over the ridge!'

Two of the men were already giving chase, scrambling up the incline at a frantic speed.

Before taking off with the girls, Archie grabbed two rocks and hurled them down the slope onto the men. As he turned to run, he heard a roar suggesting one had met its mark, but he wasn't game to look back. He scaled the hill as fast as his legs could carry him, but his feet skidded and stumbled on the rough terrain. He could hear twigs and branches breaking behind him, and the raspy breath of their pursuers. His lungs screamed for air as he clutched at roots and low branches to drag himself up the steep sections.

Ahead, the girls were nearing the crest and he rallied all his strength to make up the distance between him and the brow of the hill. But as they disappeared over the ridge, Archie felt his ankle being grabbed and wrenched from under him. He landed with a thud, hitting his head on the way down. He felt a weight like a foot in the middle of his back, then a fist grabbing at the back of Mr Peat's jacket, dragging him upwards and backwards. He tried to yell for help but wasn't sure if he'd managed it. Bile stung the back of his throat as everything spun around him in slow motion. *This is it*, he thought. *I'm dead meat.*

'We'll take him back to the boat. Throw him to the sharks.'

'Aye, we don't want a body found. But those wenches ... wait till I get me hands on them.'

Archie felt rough hands tightening around his neck. He tried to pry the fingers off but one of his arms was pinned behind him. He fought for breath as the grip constricted his windpipe. He could feel himself slipping into darkness when a distant voice came through the fog. Then, closer to his ear, he heard, 'Oi, leave off ... Someone's coming ...' He felt himself hit the ground again and the world turned black.

****

He thought he was in the tunnel again, squinting into a distant light, but couldn't see anything. He heard voices and turned but didn't recognise the faces. He sat up slowly and felt his jaw, then looked at his fingers, sticky with blood.

'Where am I?' His words echoed in his head. *Did I say that aloud?*

He had a terrible thumping in his ears. He felt hands dragging him to his feet and gruff voices urging him to take a step but he couldn't lift his foot. Words swarmed around him until he felt himself seized under each armpit and his bare feet dragging through dirt and scrub. He knew his head was slumped but he didn't have the strength to lift it. Finally he felt himself on the ground again, his head against soft earth.

Ahh … now he could just fade away … away from the pain.

****

Chapter 18

Dilemma

Jemima and Millie slid and stumbled down the western side of the ridge in a terrified frenzy, not game to stop until they fell exhausted behind some boulders.

'Thank goodness ...' Jemima panted as she recognised the place where they'd spent the night before. It was still some way below and to the right, but at least it was in sight. 'We're ... nearly there.'

Not hearing her brother crashing through the bushes as expected, she twisted to search the bush. 'Archie wasn't that far behind us, was he?'

Millie shook her head, still too breathless to speak.

Jemima stood and tilted her head but there was no hint of him tumbling down the slope at a frantic speed or, for that matter, slowly picking his way through the undergrowth. 'What could've happened? I mean, I didn't stop to look back, but I thought he was with us. And there was plenty of ground between us and those lowlife creeps, wasn't there?'

'Yeah, I heard a roar way back and thought they'd given up on the chase ... but I wasn't game to look back either. Maybe he slipped ... or something,' Millie offered. 'We'd best go and check.'

Jemima gave an exhausted groan. 'Yeah, but I'll have to rest first; my legs are so shaky and my feet are killing me.'

'Yeah, me too.' Millie rubbed at her shins as she examined her scratched, bruised feet. 'I wish we could've kept our shoes ... I suppose Mary buried them like she said.'

'Come on,' Jemima said a moment later. 'I'm worried.' As they retraced their way up the steep incline, a horrifying thought occurred to her. 'What if it's a trap? What if those sleazebags caught Archie and they're using him as bait, waiting for us to come back? Best grab something to defend ourselves,' she said, picking up a fallen branch. 'And remember, if they come at you, kick them where it hurts most.'

Dilemma

****

Reaching the top of the ridge, they peered warily down the other side. The beach where the fishing boat had been unloaded was now deserted. There were sounds of distant activity drifting from the settlement, but there was no sign of life nearby.

'They'd have to report back to work by now, or they'd cop it … so I think the scumbags are gone.' Jemima curled her lips in distaste then, inspecting a deep cut to the sole of her foot, she said, 'Geez, Mil, I don't think I can go much further.'

Millie nodded as she studied the track they'd made when bolting. 'That's the way we came,' she said pointing to flattened ferns, scuffed earth and broken twigs. 'If Archie'd fallen and hurt himself, we'd see him from here. He wouldn't leave the track, surely.'

'Come to think of it, maybe he did … Remember when he talked about heading back to Ollie, he seemed pretty confident about the way.'

'That's it, I reckon! He's taken a short cut,' Millie squinted along the ridge to her left, 'and he's already there … with Ollie.'

'That'd be right,' Jemima snarled, hands on hips. 'He's already telling Ollie everything while we're slogging it out looking for him. What a total stuff-up! We should've stayed together.'

Millie was tempted to remind Jemima it'd been *her* idea to head over the ridge for food, leaving Oliver behind, but there was no time for arguing.

'Come on … let's just find the boys and get the hell out of here.'

****

As they neared the rock-shelter, a mob of grazing rock-wallabies bounded away at their approach. Something wasn't right. And as they rounded the outcrop, their fear was confirmed.

'This is the right place, isn't it?' Jemima looked around wildly, before her eyes settled on Oliver's twine loop on the ground. 'What the …?'

'It looks like a noose, doesn't it? Is it a sign, do you think?' Millie crouched beside the twine. 'It's pointing downhill, to the water.'

Jemima was already edging away. 'Come on; let's go.'

'Wait,' Millie said as she scrambled out of Mary's shift and threw it under the rock-shelter. Jemima did the same. 'It's a relief to get that thing off. It's slowed me down, bunching up around my legs.'

'Yeah, me too. Geez, they're so ripped it'll look like a dog's dragged them off the clothesline. Come on; we've wasted enough time already. Let's get to the water and hope we find the boys, then get as far from here as we can.' Her voice held a panic she couldn't disguise.

****

They had no idea how much time had passed when they finally stumbled onto a narrow beach. Limping to a shallow rock pool, they soaked their lacerated feet and then collapsed onto a low stone ledge. Neither of them wanted to discuss the fact they hadn't seen any sign of the boys.

Eventually Jemima recovered enough to take in their surrounds. 'This is familiar … It's the same beach we found after we left the tunnel. Remember? I'm sure it's the same place.'

Millie sat up, looked around and shrugged. She was still too shattered for conversation.

'I remember looking along this shoreline for the bridge or the Opera House … for any signs of life, but it was deserted,' Jemima persisted.

'Well, it's not now. Look …' Millie pointed to five or six canoes across the water; their occupants were fishing with lines. 'We should hide.' Her heart was hammering in her chest. She knew it was too late; they'd been spotted. One of the vessels was coming towards them.

'Okay, what now? I'm too scared to think.'

They saw an arm rise and they responded with the same gesture. Then a warm female voice called, 'Hello,' and Jemima felt her shoulders relax a little. Once they were within easy speaking distance the young occupant inspected them with curiosity. Jemima imagined the weird, bedraggled sight they must be presenting to the stranger.

'Um … we are lost,' Jemima said, deciding to use the same phrase that had worked before. She hoped the young woman understood.

'Yes,' she replied simply and continued studying them. Jemima was wondering what to say next when the woman got out of her vessel, waded to the beach and pulled it onto the sand. Then, sitting near them, she said out of the blue, 'I am Boorong. I think you know Oliver?'

Millie's dirt-streaked face lit up with wide-eyed hope. 'Yes!' she cried, echoing Jemima's response. 'Yes, he's my brother … You know where he is?' She looked into the young woman's face with searching eyes, her hands together as if in prayer.

'Go-Mo-Ra,' Boorong replied, pointing in the direction she'd paddled from earlier. 'I can take you, but only one.' She held up a single finger then, crossing to her canoe, she spread her hands, inviting Millie to check its contents. 'My nawi is full.'

When Millie joined her, she saw it was packed with food and equipment: woven net bags with paperbark rolls, twine, spun fishing lines and shell fishhooks. There were also various wooden bowls with berries, yams and other food. But what caught Millie's attention were the containers of whitish clay.

'*Ta-boa* – clay to paint face and body,' Boorong explained. She pushed a finger into the clay and then made a white line on her cheek. 'For our corroboree,' she said, her face beaming.

'Wow,' Millie nodded with genuine interest, but her mind was racing with the pros and cons of this stranger's offer. It would mean getting into her flimsy-looking canoe and heading into the wilderness, to who knows where. It *seemed* a kind gesture, but it could be a trap. Then again, she had to find Ollie.

After meeting Jemima's probing stare, she gave a quick nod. 'Thank you, Boorong. I um ...'

'What!' Jemima spluttered, cutting her off. 'But what about ...' She faltered, not knowing how to continue; her thoughts were muddled. She shook her head, trying to clear it.

By now another young woman had paddled across the water and pulled her nawi onto the sand. She nodded to them and spoke privately with Boorong. Millie heard them say 'Oliver' several times but didn't understand the rest of their exchange. They seemed to be devising a plan.

After several minutes of discussion, they began moving the containers of clay and some of the food from Boorong's nawi to the other vessel.

'Now I can take two,' Boorong said, waving her hand to a space where they could sit.

Jemima was considering her reply when the fishing vessel they'd watched being unloaded hours earlier came into view near the headland. Boorong followed her tense gaze.

'Boat of gov'nor,' she explained but then, seeing their frowns, she added, 'But Mr Bryant, he goes fishing in that boat. He is the gov'nor's chief fisherman.'

'Well, some men in that boat chased us ... and,' Jemima's voice was quivering now, 'and ... and they may have killed my brother!' she blurted, casting a terrified look at the boat. She could feel herself losing control now that she'd put her fear about Archie into words; her whole body began trembling.

Millie also felt shaky at the thought of coming face to face with those men again. Seeing the boat and believing the men were still after them was too much. The tears she'd been fighting back now spilled silently down her cheeks. She dabbed at them, trying to hold herself together.

'No, not Mr Bryant ... he is no killer,' Boorong said, affected by their distress. 'He's our friend ... we fish with him many times ... He is a convict man, but no killer.' Then, narrowing her eyes as she watched the boat disappear down the harbour, she said, 'But other white men … they kill to hide their wicked plans.'

Jemima was tempted to tell her what they'd witnessed but decided to keep it to herself. Instead, she looked about wildly, searching for a way to express her anxiety for Archie.

'My brother,' she said wringing her hands. 'I must look for Archie. I can't leave.' She felt clammy and wiped the sweat from her face with the back of her hand. 'He is near Tar-Ra … I think.'

'I think you need food and water,' Boorong said, looking from one to the other. Jemima nodded, knowing she was so weak she could hardly sit up anymore. Next to her, Millie's sniffles turned to sobs.

'Ba-do,' Boorong called to her companion, who was still rearranging her gear. The young woman brought water for them and, as they gratefully gulped it down, Boorong said, 'Do not fear. Today *my* brother is there … at Tar-Ra. He is hunting *wir-ri-ga*.' She spread her arms, indicating something long.

'What? But …' Jemima's words tapered off; her head was spinning.

'My brother will know if bad men come to Tar-Ra. He will help Archie.'

'But …' Jemima bit her lip. She wanted to say *but bad men* did *come with their* wicked plan – but there'd been no sign of Boorong's brother or his brave deeds. But she didn't say anything; she didn't have the strength for any more talking. There was no option but to go with Boorong. Jemima gave a tight smile and thanked her, but she was still full of dread.

****

Chapter 19

Go-Mo-Ra camp

The girls clambered into Boorong's nawi with feelings of both gratitude and apprehension. As they glided away from the shore, Jemima gazed up the slope, trying to reassure herself she was doing the right thing. *Archie's okay; he's somewhere safe*, she said over and over in her mind.

Millie saw her cousin's sad, darting eyes and squeezed her arm. They both knew they were too exhausted to go searching for Archie, and that neither of them would bring up their fears about the men in the fishing boat.

What had those men hidden that made them so desperate? Millie wondered with a shudder. Did it warrant murder? Surely, they wouldn't hang around if they had Archie on the boat? She tried to stop thinking about it. *At least we'll see Oliver soon*, she assured herself, trying to divert her thoughts.

As Boorong paddled further from the bank she called out to the other females still fishing near the opposite shore. Getting their attention, she jabbed her finger upstream and, cupping her hands to her mouth, she called 'Go-Mo-Ra.' And the others waved back.

Go-Mo-Ra – that's where Oliver is – Millie breathed a sigh of relief. It felt so good to take the weight off her aching feet, and to be heading away from Sydney. The bark vessel carrying them smoothly through the water felt like a refuge. She put her hand over the side and dangled her fingers into the cool water. She watched Boorong, sitting ahead of her, put her paddles aside and blow life into a smouldering fire positioned on a flat clay pad in front of her. Then she took several small fish from a net bag and placed them into the flames. Millie felt her mouth watering as they began to sizzle. Except for a piece of dry bread, they'd had nothing to eat for nearly twenty-four hours. Boorong flicked the cooked fish to the side of the fire and onto folded paperbark. She handed one to Millie and another to Jemima, who began breaking pieces of fish off with her fingers. Millie had never tasted anything so fresh and delicious.

She was on her second mouthful when the sound of splashing made her twist to see a flock of pelicans taking off for flight directly from the water. As they flapped their enormous wings and lifted into the air, the women fishing in their nawis some distance behind began singing. Boorong joined in the vocals. Millie couldn't understand the words but found herself smiling as she hummed the melody and saw Jemima doing the same. The repeated chorus sounded like:

'Gnoo-roo-me, ta-tie, na-tie, na-tie ...'

Boorong paused to explain that whenever they saw pelicans in flight, the women shared that song. It was a sight and sound experience that made Millie's throat choke with emotion. As she looked skywards at the brilliant, white-breasted birds hovering above, it seemed as if they were lingering deliberately to be part of the shared experience. Millie felt immersed in the moment too. It was exhilarating and calming at the same time: the sky, the water, the birds and human beings all seemed as one. Finally, the birds rose higher and flew into the distance in a v-formation, and the singing faded, leaving the low hum of insects and the chittering of smaller birds to waft from bushland along the banks.

With the soft whirr of nature and the rhythmic motion of the vessel in time with Boorong's paddling, Millie and Jemima became drowsy and were soon lulled into a gentle doze, losing any sense of time.

In the quietness, Boorong's thoughts drifted again to the strangers' appearance. Their bodies moved awkwardly, as if they ate much and moved little. As they'd climbed into the nawi, she'd noticed their soft, smooth feet. Although shoeless now, and with fresh cuts and scratches, it appeared their soles had rarely touched bare earth before today. At first she'd thought all their toenails and fingernails were covered in dried blood, but it didn't wash off in the water, so she decided it was some kind of body paint. As Nanberry had said, they were like fish out of water.

Minutes later, Boorong startled them both when she called over her shoulder, 'We are here now.'

As they drifted past a huge rock jutting into the water, the sight of Oliver sitting alone beside a small fire greeted them. And on seeing them in the nawi, he began waving excitedly.

****

'Where's Archie?' Oliver called out before the girls had even joined him by the fireside. Once seated, they began filling him in on what had happened since leaving him that morning. It seemed a long time since their separation from Archie. It was difficult to recall details but Oliver kept plying them with questions.

'We'll tell you more tomorrow, Ollie,' said Millie flatly. 'I can't keep talking about it now.'

Boorong, aware of the girls' distress, said, 'My brother will help Archie. Do not worry.' Then turning to Jemima, as if to change the subject, Boorong posed a question she'd wanted to ask since first seeing her. 'Do you watch the stars like Mr Dawes?' she said, pointing to the tattoo of the Southern Cross on Jemima's forehead. Jemima's fingers sprang to her hairline.

'Oh, um …' She'd completely forgotten about her tattoo – with no mirror, she hadn't seen her face for what seemed like an eternity.

Boorong smiled and continued. 'Mr Dawes built a place he calls *observatory* – to watch stars. It has a roof like this.' She drew a conical shape in the sand with a stick. 'And it moves around.' She gestured above her head to show the roof revolving. 'And … opens so he can see the stars.' Boorong posed as if holding a telescope to the sky.

Jemima dipped her head, remembering the building with the pointy white canvas roof, at Dawes Point.

'I know *those* stars.' Boorong pointed again at Jemima's tattoo.

Jemima's hand went to her brow again. She remembered getting the tattoo – without her parents' permission – after she'd learned of their planned separation. She'd sat on the step of their farmhouse porch feeling confused, choked and angry that they were moving to the city. She'd looked up into the night sky to see the stars twinkling back at her. It had felt reassuring – like she wasn't alone.

'We call these stars the Southern Cross.' Jemima touched her forehead again. She was glad to talk about something other than their day's ordeal. 'I got this – *tattoo* we call it – because the Southern Cross reminds me of home.'

'My name means star,' Boorong announced as Jemima's fingers traced her tattoo. 'Those stars are part of *War-re-wul* ... Mr Dawes calls it the Milky Way.'

'War-re-wul,' Jemima repeated. 'I'll remember that.'

'I must go now – for the corroboree.' Boorong rose to leave. 'Afterwards I will stay with others at Bennelong's house or the gov'nor's, but I will come tomorrow with news of your brother, Archie.' Then pointing from Jemima's feet to nearby paperbark trees, she said, 'Bark from that tree will heal your feet.'

'Thank you, Boorong.' Jemima stood too and watched Boorong get into her nawi and paddle out of sight.

As Millie and Oliver were dozing beside the fire, Jemima sat quietly staring into the flames, thinking about her tattoo and how she'd been heckled about it at her new city high school. The kids had called her a racist because of it and, not getting why, she'd checked the internet to learn that the Southern Cross *was* used as a racist symbol by some. From then on she'd hidden her tattoo under her thick, curly fringe. But yesterday – was it really only yesterday? – she'd thought, *Stuff them*. She wasn't going to let them turn a cool symbol into an ugly meaning, and she'd shaved her head to flaunt her Southern Cross. It had made her feel strong.

Her mind drifted back to a conversation with her father one evening after a TV show on astronomy. They'd been sitting on the verandah step when he'd looked up at the night sky and said, 'You know, we're all made of stardust, Jem.' She'd thought about that often. Oh, she missed her father.

And she missed Archie – she felt helpless sitting here unable to help him. She wished she hadn't put him down so much. She could be mean sometimes.

****

It was impossible to know how much time had passed without her phone, so Jemima told herself it didn't matter. They had no choice but to wait for morning – when hopefully they'd meet up with Archie and head home. The campfire flickered and hissed, radiating a soft glow into the leafy canopy suspended from the darkness above. On the log beside her, Millie was doodling in the earth with a stick.

'You okay now, Mil?'

'Sort of … I'm trying not to think about what's out there, in the bush.' Millie looked up to the night sky and Jemima followed her gaze. 'Look at it, Jem – the Milky Way. I've never seen stars like this before.'

'Yeah, it's pretty awesome. Boorong called it War-re-wul.' Jemima pointed and traced imaginary lines between stars in the brightest part of the Milky Way. 'See the Southern Cross? It's like a kite shape really, isn't it?'

'Mm, I wonder if Archie's looking at the stars, wherever he is?'

'I hope so.' Jemima sighed, feeling bleak again. She looked across at Oliver's hunched outline. He seemed cocooned in his own thoughts. His foot was still swathed in a paperbark bandage, propped on another log. 'What're you thinking about, Ollie?'

'Something Boorong said to me, about the settlement at

Parramatta. Seems more settlers are moving out there along the river, clearing the land for crops … It's not right cos …'

'Not right? Why not? They *need* food, Ollie, and they can't grow much around here. Look at this!' Jemima grabbed a handful of dusty earth, letting it run through her fingers. 'They're practically starving in Sydney Cove. We've seen it first-hand.'

'But *why* are they starving, Jem? How come Boorong's people managed to find enough food for thousands of years without flattening forests?'

'Far out, Ollie! You're the one who pulled a face about eating wild berries this morning. You said you wanted proper food, remember?'

'Yeah, well, I've changed my mind, okay. Anyway, the point is … since the Brits settled along the river, Boorong's people had to move away … cos *their* food's gone …'

'But –' Jemima tried to interrupt but Oliver put his hand up.

'… cos the British government's handing out land … more than one hundred acres per officer. And convicts get land too, when their time's up … See, the thing is, they're handing out land that's *not theirs*.' Oliver stressed the last two words, his expression intense in the firelight. 'And, like I said, it's not right.'

'Well, you tell me, Ollie, what's Governor Phillip supposed to do? They thought more ships were coming with food, but none did … for years. So, like I said, what were they supposed to do? Tell me that. They were starving – they still are!'

'Jem, I'm just saying … see it from Boorong's point. She gave the governor a message that her people weren't happy with so many settlers along the river. And you know what he did?'

He paused for Jemima's reply but she just stared at him. She wasn't used to her younger cousin being so deep and meaningful.

'He sent more soldiers there …' Oliver opened his arms to imply the injustice of it.

'Well, you didn't hear Mary Mullins's story today … you didn't *see* how she lives.' She thumbed in the direction of Sydney Cove.

'She didn't *choose* to come here – she was forced. And they're stranded – they can't just get a plane home. The governor can't sail everyone back to Old England, can he? I mean, what would *you* do if you had his job? Hey? What would you do in his shoes?' Jemima had worked herself up.

Oliver and Millie looked at her with concern.

Oliver was sick of her ranting, but at the risk of drawing the argument out, he said, 'He could listen, for a start. He could listen to the people who lived here long before he arrived.'

Jemima met his gaze and let out a long sigh to calm herself. 'Look, I'm sorry about raving on … My nerves are rattled. I'm worried about Archie … I just wish I knew he was okay.'

'So do we, Jem … He's on our minds too. But arguing between ourselves isn't helping.'

****

Chapter 20

Night Visit

Millie was sitting on a log, watching smoke spiral into the darkness. The breeze lifted, sending a waft towards her; the smell of smouldering leaves tickled her nose. She stared into the embers, seeing shapes in the glowing coals. She imagined an owl's head in the orange cinders, black spots for its eyes. Small flames sputtered and curled like tongues licking at the logs.

The heat was comforting on her face but, behind, the air felt chilly against her neck. She resisted the temptation to look over her shoulder into the shadows. She turned instead to Oliver and Jemima, huddled in conversation beside the fire. Smoke gently billowed over them and Jemima waved her hand absent-mindedly into the haze. *Thank goodness they've done with arguing.*

Possum growls erupted from the darkness and Jemima looked up for her reaction. Millie smiled, remembering her resolve to *be brave* and gave her the thumbs up. Oliver grinned as if to say *All good.*

'Sleep time, I think,' Jemima said drowsily as Millie and Oliver stretched and yawned.

Oliver began shuffling himself into a comfortable position by the fire and Millie closed her heavy eyelids. As she opened them and leaned into another stretch, she sensed movement to her left. She twisted around slightly and waited. It must be her imagination, she told herself; no-one else had reacted. Oliver was propped on one elbow, staring into the embers. Jemima was busy mounding up bracken fern to form her pillow and arranging the kangaroo skins Boorong had left them.

Millie told herself the movement was just the swishing of leaves on the fringe of the clearing. She decided to ignore it, taking a deep breath to bring her imagination under control. But there it was again – this time more distinct. She turned her head slowly towards the forest to convince herself there was nothing there. But there was. She took a sharp breath in, hardly able to move.

A dark shape was silently approaching the clearing through the undergrowth. Millie opened her mouth but no sound came. The form stayed low until it reached the edge of the grove then slowly straightened, sending eerie shadows against the tree trunks. Panic rushed through her but, like in a dream, she couldn't move. Whatever it was, its features were hidden by long tangled fur – or was it hair? Millie tried to blink, dragging herself back to reality but was hypnotised by the sight.

As the figure edged closer and paused, hands reached out as if to say *Don't scream*. Then the long hair fell back to reveal frightened eyes. Pale lips tried to form a smile. The face belonged to a young white woman. The fear gripping Millie fell away – instead she felt a wave of pity for the creature, who seemed more afraid than her.

With a finger to her lips, the young woman drew closer to Millie and sat at an arm's length from her on the log. Millie slowly turned and looked at her. The stranger's face, framed by coarse sun-bleached hair, was smudged and sunburnt. But her eyes were expressive, her features not unpleasant. Her body was draped in rags, and she was clutching an animal skin around her shoulders.

'Hello,' the visitor whispered, as if she was trying out the word.

'Hello,' Millie replied and immediately saw the woman's shoulders relax. Millie looked to her right but the others seemed unaware of the visitor. Oliver was already snoring, Jemima facing away. It seemed strange that they hadn't heard the woman approach or felt her presence.

'I … I shouldn't be here, I know,' the woman whispered and wrung her hands. 'Downright dangerous, it is … but I just had to.'

Millie was surprised by her accent; it seemed out of place in this wilderness. She sounded like their neighbour in Windmill Street. She didn't know what to say next, so she just waited.

'When I heard youse was here I just had to come,' the woman said in a nervous burst.

What does she mean, 'heard we were here'? Millie thought, feeling panic again.

'I had to come,' the stranger repeated, 'to hear me own lingo again, and for ... old times' sake.' Her tone pleaded understanding.

But Millie wasn't listening. All she could focus on was that their presence was known. Her chest tightened. *How long will it be before soldiers come bursting through the undergrowth demanding to know who we are? Worse still, what if we're seized, forced into chains and taken to Sydney Cove as prisoners?*

'Um, how did you know we were here?' Millie demanded, looking around. She should let the others know, tell them they had to get away. She was about to call out when she felt the woman's hand on her arm, squeezing tight.

'I should've said first up,' she whispered hurriedly. 'None of them knows you're here.' She nodded in the direction of the British settlement.

'Well, how do *you* know?' Millie's tone was distrustful now, even nasty.

'I don't live in Sydney, luv,' she blurted. 'I escaped ... a long time ago now.'

'Escaped? How?' Millie demanded again. 'How'd you survive, out here by yourself?'

'Same as you, luv,' the woman replied, without looking at Millie. 'The Eora helped me.' Again, Millie didn't know what to say, but the woman's story seemed credible now. She turned to look at her, questions tumbling through her mind.

'Eora? The natives?'

'Course, *they* know you're here, luv. They don't miss anything, you know.' The woman picked up a twig and doodled in the earth around her bare feet. Millie noticed the thick calluses, the ingrained dirt between her toes and in the creases around her ankles.

'So why've you taken the risk now ... to come here?' Millie

asked in a softer voice.

'Cos I still get lonely for me own, like, and I just wanna talk me own lingo for a bit … And I thought youse might have news from home – about me family and the like.'

'No, sorry … we don't know where home is right now.' Millie said it like a confession, feeling a sudden connection with the stranger.

'Well, I won't ask no questions, luv – unless of course you wanna talk.'

She guesses we're hiding something, Millie thought, glad she didn't have to explain.

'I'm Millie,' she said turning fully to the woman. And, on a whim, she added, 'Are you from London?' The woman's head jerked up in surprise, making Millie jump.

'Oi, how'd you know that, then?' The woman's eyes shone in the firelight'. Without waiting, she said, 'I'm Ann. Me full name's Ann Smith, but I haven't said it in years. Eh, it's good to have a chat.'

'So you're a convict?' Millie immediately regretted her question as a cloud darkened Ann's face.

'Con-vict,' Ann sounded each syllable. 'Huh – haven't said that word in years either. I *was* a convict.'

Millie saw bitterness etched into Ann's face.

'Wanna know why I got sent here, to the end of the earth? Me crime?' She glanced in the direction of the trees but again didn't wait for reply. In fact, it was almost as if Millie was no longer there; Ann was reliving a deeply felt injustice.

'I was tried at the Old Bailey, London, for nicking a pewter pint pot …'

Millie wasn't sure what that was, but pictured a large metal mug, like in olden-day tavern scenes in movies. *What would a pint pot be worth?* she wondered.

'Valued at sixpence,' Ann continued. 'Six pennies,' she said, slowing her words.

That's not much, Millie thought. *There has to be more to it.*

'I was sitting in the White Horse Inn, Bishopsgate, with me

pennyworth of beer in front of me – I'd already had a few, mind you. And I thought to meself, if I just slip this empty pot into me basket, I might get something for it later on. And so I did. Then, later on, I was in the street – and remember I'd had a few pints by then – and I thought me cloak was covering me basket. Anyways, Mr Dodson, the publican, comes out looking for his pewter pot – and the baker's coming up the street past me, and he points and says, "It's in her basket."'

'What happened then?' Millie imagined Ann dropping the basket and running through cobblestoned streets, chased by the publican, the baker and a line of constables. Ann let out a sigh.

'I, um … I said it were someone else's basket. But that didn't work cos it weren't me first time, see.' Ann glanced at Millie, her mouth twisted. 'But I thought at worst I'd cop a flogging and that'd be that, you know.'

How strange to talk of a flogging in such a matter-of-fact way … as if it was normal. But Ann continued her story as if it was.

'Cos it were only petty larceny – under a shillingsworth.'

Millie guessed it meant a minor crime. 'So, how come …'

'Well, the day of me trial, the judge decided … oh, how'd he put it?' Ann searched the darkness, trying to recall the words that changed her life.

'To set an example … that's how he put it.' She hesitated, clearing her throat. 'And then he said, "The ruling is … you will be transported for seven years."' Ann groaned, clutching the animal skin tightly around her shoulders. 'Just like that, he said it – as if it were nothing really.' A choking sound escaped her.

'Surely …' Millie began, but saw Ann was still reliving those moments in court, so they sat quietly absorbed in their own thoughts.

Millie recalled kids at school showing off the designer clothes they'd pinched. She'd done it herself – pocketed a bottle of perfume – on a dare. She tried to imagine being hauled before a court, then banished to the other side of the earth … forever … as penalty.

'I couldn't take it in,' Ann whispered, shaking her head. 'I knew it meant being sent away, far from me home and me ma and … But I didn't know what it *really* meant, not till I were locked below deck like a caged animal, heading to the ends of the earth. That's when it sank in – that I'd never see them again.'

'I can't imagine …' was all Millie managed before Ann continued, talking over her words.

'It were on that voyage, I made up me mind I were escaping. And I told them so – the women in that dingy hole with me. And I told them in charge too … They didn't believe me of course.' Ann gave a short chuckle at her own bravado.

'But you did! You actually did it!' Millie was aware of sounding too upbeat, but Ann's rebellion against such injustice seemed a triumph in Millie's mind now.

'It weren't that easy, luv,' Ann said quietly. 'I were scared witless.'

'I bet.' Millie looked at the forest encircling them – the seemingly endless wilderness – and imagined being out there completely alone. *How has this small-framed white woman survived by herself out there?*

Millie felt a chill go through her. She stood and went to the fireside, placing small logs on the dwindling flames and fanning it to life. Then she settled back for the rest of the story, pleased it was just the two of them.

****

'Go on, then; tell me about your escape.'

'When we finally got to Sydney Cove, all we could see was wilderness – there weren't a road or building in sight. It was so flamin' hot and weird sounds were coming out of them woods – whirring and screeching. And the air smelt … different. Even with all the buzzing and squawking, the woods seemed so still. O' course, we didn't know what man-eating beasts might be in that forest yet.'

Night Visit

Millie imagined taking that first step onto dry land after months at sea – not knowing what lurked behind the trees. She imagined herself inside a flimsy tent that first night, wondering what might be prowling outside. She shuddered at the thought. *What possessed Ann to take off into the wild?*

'But why …? I mean, didn't you have second thoughts about going off on your own?' Millie was eager to hear the details.

'Oh, maybe – when I thought about them cannibal rumours.' Ann chuckled through her words, then her expression became serious. 'But it was when they got us women lined up and they were looking us up and down, I thought *I'm not staying round here to be a slave*. Of course, I waited till they was all busy looking t'other way.'

'I planned on headin' to Botany Bay cos everyone knew about the French ships there, and I thought I'd stow meself on board. But of course I got lost … soon as I left the settlement.'

Millie shuddered again.

'Aye, I haven't thought about this for a long time, but I were scared witless. I walked 'n walked till me blisters were red raw. It were stinking hot that day and me water soon ran out. I remember eating me last bits o' bread and when it got dark – and the forest came alive with grunts and scratchin' sounds – I prayed that I would be left alone. I must've drifted off cos when I woke it was light, and a circle of natives was standing there looking down at me.'

'I bet you were scared witless?' Millie decided she'd adopt Ann's expression.

'I was, cos I didn't understand a word they said, and they looked fierce to me then. But they was kind, giving me water and some cooked fish. They made signs for me to go with them – and I did. And …'

'How long have you …?'

'Don't know, luv.' Ann shrugged. 'Time don't matter when you're free – it's *always* now.'

Millie looked at Ann's profile: the determined set of her chin, her strong-minded gaze and the resolute line of her mouth, and admired her. She'd seen life in Sydney Cove earlier that day – she'd seen the hovels. She'd tasted their awful food – salted meat, kept for years in barrels. She'd seen the chains and the mean punishment. She'd seen how their days revolved around endless backbreaking work that seemed so pointless to her now, as she sat here in the gentle firelight.

There was so much she wanted to ask Ann about her life now. *Hasn't it been rough? Hasn't it been lonely?* Clearly she missed her own culture; that's what had brought her here tonight. She opened her mouth to broach the subject but Ann cut in, warding off questions.

'Come on,' she said. 'Let's go for a swim.'

Millie stared at her, wide-eyed with disbelief.

'It's pitch black out there.'

'Not when you get there,' Ann said with a mysterious air. 'Come on.'

Before there was time to object, Ann was on her feet. And, as if in a daze, Millie followed her into the darkness.

****

Chapter 21

Sky and Water

Ann moved quickly through the undergrowth with Millie struggling to keep up. She clutched the front of her shirt with both hands as if that would somehow provide protection from whatever lurked beyond the narrow track. She looked over her shoulder, wondering what had possessed her to leave the camp site. There was no moonlight, though there was enough starlight to see trees and bushes outlined against the sky and that their pathway ran parallel to the water. Ann stopped ahead of her and half turned.

'Dingo is waiting for us – don't be bothered by her.' When Millie gasped, Ann said, 'Just let her get used to you ... see you won't hurt her.'

'Me? Hurt her ...?' A second later Millie saw the animal beside the track watching her. Its ears alert, the white fur of its chest and paws contrasted with its tan body. Its penetrating stare made Millie paralysed with fear.

'Com'on,' Ann said to the animal, and Millie was relieved to see it spring ahead, leading the way.

'Is it your pet?'

'No, we just look out for each other. She comes and goes as she likes.'

Ann veered off the track to a stretch of sand edging the water where a backdrop of rock face sheltered the little cove from the wind. As soon as they reached the bank, Ann pulled her frock over her head and waded into the water till she was waist deep. Millie watched her lean into the darkness and propel her body forwards until only her head was visible. It seemed the most natural thing in the world.

Millie looked around to see Dingo watching her intently. She didn't like being alone on the shore so she stripped off her outer clothes and waded into the water, feeling it lap at her ankles. Looking down, she imagined the sand swishing around her feet, her toes digging in for balance. Goosebumps covered her arms and she let the shiver waft over her. The water was cool but not icy, not unpleasant. She edged her way in feeling the water creep up her legs. The ebb and flow of small waves now gently caressed her thighs.

She stole a look behind to see Dingo on the beach, relaxed, with her chin resting on the sand. Millie turned back, searching the water for Ann but couldn't see her. She felt a rush of panic, then heard a ripple a short distance away and saw Ann's head bob above the surface. Millie was waist deep now. Then, sinking down to her shoulders and stretching her arms out, she pushed off from the bottom, over to Ann. The water swayed like a satin sheet between them. To float through the darkness was a strangely invigorating sensation. When she reached Ann she let out a sound of childlike delight.

'Now just let yourself fall back and look at the sky,' Ann said as she leaned back into the water to float on its surface. Without a word Millie imitated her, easing onto her back, allowing her legs to lift, closing her eyes and letting the water support her and carry her along like a leaf.

When she opened her eyes she couldn't believe the vision above her. She'd had a taste of the night sky at the camp site but here, looking up from the water, it was dazzling. It seemed to be alive. The Milky Way seemed like a great sweep of snowflakes merging into a luminous cloud spun with swirls. A million stars twinkled in tones of blue-white and golden yellow, like a meadow of wildflowers. The sky wasn't just above her; it was *around* her. She was immersed in it, just as she was immersed in the water.

'This is the best feeling … this isn't possible where I come from …' As Millie said the words, a bizarre thought occurred to her. *This is where I come from – I'm in Darling Harbour, not far from Sydney's*

CBD ... but here now I'm seeing it without city lights – before light pollution made the stars hardly visible. It was a sad thought that brought her back to earth.

'I want to go back to the camp site now, Ann.'

Millie let her feet sink and her body tilt upright. The spell was broken. A breeze sprang up, licking the water's surface into little waves. Millie quivered.

As Ann turned to her and nodded, the sound of rhythmic clapping drifted around the headland with the change of air current.

Millie tilted her head. 'What's that?'

'That'll be the corroboree – a gathering for song and dance – it's a way yonder. Com'on then, we'll go back.' Ann was already heading back to the beach, where Dingo stood in anticipation.

Ann rubbed herself dry with her kangaroo skin and donned her frock, while Millie ducked behind a bush and peeled off her wet undies to slip back into her shorts and shirt. As she did, something fell out of the pocket and brushed against her leg. She froze for a second thinking it was a creepy crawly but realised it was Tench's feather quill. As she bent to pick it up, her finger touched something else – something round and metallic – *a coin?* She returned to Ann and held it up – a black disc outlined against the star-studded night sky.

'There ain't many coins to be found around here, luv – you'd best keep that for luck.'

Millie slipped it into her pocket with Tench's quill. Then they sat on the sand – with Dingo parked between them – while the breeze dried their hair.

****

As they retraced their steps, Millie questioned whether this was really happening to her, but the damp clothes dangling from her hand – and the coin in her pocket – were real. She thought about their earlier conversation, about Ann's life, about her choices.

'Where will you go now, Ann?'

'My friends are night fishing now. We'll meet up and head off; our camp's away across the water.'

'Do you think you would've survived, on your own in the bush?'

'S'pose I'll never know – probably not.'

'I think it's the same for us. We'd be starving without Nanberry and Boorong's help. Not like some white men who chased us just cos we saw them. They were up to no good ... those white men. Convicts, I bet.' She spat the words.

'Ah, just remember good and bad comes in all skin tones, luv. I've seen it; believe me. And, just cos someone's branded a convict don't make them evil. Remember that ...'

Millie felt embarrassed; she *had* judged all convicts as bad without knowing their stories.

'I will, now I've met you – and Mary Mullins too. She told us her ma's story. And she tried to help us – gave us bread and lent us clothes – but we took off to dodge getting caught.'

'Was that when the men chased youse?'

'No, we got away without being seen at the settlement. But closer to Dawes Point we saw men burying something near the waterfront, and they spotted us – and came after us. Jem and I got away but they may've grabbed my cousin, Archie ... we don't know. I don't want to think about it.'

'Ee, bad things happen; we can't pretend otherwise.'

That wasn't what Millie wanted to hear. *Poor Archie!*

'Boorong said her brother would help Archie if he saw him ... but ...'

They were nearing the camp site and paused to say their goodbyes. Then Ann headed back along the track with Dingo leading the way.

Millie tiptoed into camp and settled herself beside the fire, just as she'd been when Ann arrived. Jemima and Oliver were asleep but she felt wide awake, her mind abuzz with Ann's mysterious presence, her pint pot, her verdict, her ship voyage, her escape,

Sky and Water

night swimming, the Milky Way, Dingo … and Archie.
Where are you, Archie?

****

Chapter 22

Archie

Archie turned onto his side and blinked his eyes open. He felt a rush of panic, thinking he'd lost his sight, but slowly shapes formed. He saw two figures sitting in the dark beside a small fire. He tried to speak but only a grunt erupted from his throat. The shapes swivelled around to him and he saw their features partly illuminated by the flames: a white man and a native man, in their early twenties.

He lifted his head, but it thumped violently with the effort. 'Where am I?' His voice sounded so croaky he wasn't sure he'd formed the words properly. He tried to moisten his lips with his tongue.

The white man offered him water, which he swallowed with difficulty; his throat was incredibly sore, and his neck felt restricted. He put a hand to his throat and felt some sort of binding around it. Again, panic surged through him. *Am I bound like a prisoner?*

'What's going on?' he croaked. 'What happened?'

'We're hoping you can tell us,' the white man said in a strange, harsh accent.

Archie's mind was fuzzy, but he tried to recall his movements that day. He shuddered as vague, frightening images flashed before him. He couldn't remember details but knew he'd been in danger. He tried to move, but his arms and legs felt like weights. He let his head flop back to the ground knowing he was at the mercy of these two men, whoever they were.

They were both watching him, waiting for him to speak. 'I don't remember,' he said simply. 'My head hurts.'

'Aye, and you'd know why if you could see it,' the same man said. 'Found you over yonder, we did. Heard shouting and went to check. Just as well, or you'd be done for. Saw the old lags take off.'

'Who?'

'Oh, I'll not name names but there's them that have a plan hatching. We knew they was up to something along by the water there, but turned a blind eye – it don't pay to meddle – till we heard the disturbance. Cos, see, everyone about here was meant to be at the parade ground for the flogging.'

Flogging? It was coming to back to him through a haze – he'd been there, at a flogging. He had an image of gooey, mashed-up pink flesh; he could hear the wet slap against the man's back. *But why, who?*

Someone else was there with him … watching the flogging. He tried to focus, but it was just beyond his reach. He wanted to close his eyes and fade back into oblivion, but his mind wouldn't stop questioning now. He wanted to ask these men why *they* weren't at the flogging, if *everyone* was meant to be there. But his instinct told him to say nothing – or as little as possible – till he knew why he was here, in the darkness with these strangers. He still hadn't fully seen their faces.

'So, what *do* you remember, then?' It was the white man still questioning him. 'Where are you from, cos we know you ain't from here?'

'Sorry, I can't remember.' Archie shook his head but it throbbed with the movement. He tried to loosen the binding around his neck and managed to push his fingers under it. The skin at his throat felt broken and raw; his fingers came out tacky. He realised it was a type of paperbark bandage, like he'd seen covering someone's foot, but couldn't fathom who, when or where.

'Can I ask …'

'As you wish, but will you eat first?', invited the native man.

Archie hadn't realised how hungry he was till the mention of food. He nodded weakly and pushed his way onto his elbow though every part of his body hurt.

'This is good for you,' the man said as he cut portions of meat off a chunk by the fire and brought it to him on a tin plate.

Archie bit into a piece.

'Mm, chicken,' he said, licking the oil from his lips, making the man erupt with cheery laughter.

'Maybe *like* chicken,' he said. 'But it is *wir-ri-ga* from our hunt today.'

Archie looked more closely at the long lump of roasted meat beside the fire and decided it must be goanna.

'Tastes good,' he said, already feeling slightly better. 'Thanks.'

'I am Ballooderry.' The man came forwards to shake hands.

Archie lifted his arm up with difficulty. He could see the young man's face now and felt relieved by his kind, open smile. He had strong, broad shoulders and handsome features. The white man offered his hand in the same manner; his hand felt rough and callused in Archie's limp hold.

'I'm Wilson. They call me the wild, idle one back there.' He thumbed over his shoulder towards the settlement. Archie saw at once why he'd earned the label 'wild'. His rustic, sun-hardened features and rugged manner confirmed his liking for outdoor living. Raising a furrowed brow, Wilson added, 'Wild I may be, but never idle.'

'Hello.' Archie dipped his head slightly to them both. 'How come ...?' he tried forming a question which Wilson finished for him.

'How come they let me hunt with Ballooderry and his mob? That's what you're wondering, aye?'

Archie nodded, though it hadn't been his question.

'Truth is ... me job's everything from carving rocks to lugging bricks, but hunting's what I'm good at and they know it. Anyway, I'll be a free man soon cos me time's nearly done, see, and I'll be leavin' that miserable place behind ...' Wilson let out a harsh laugh as he recalled the words Judge Collins had hurled at him recently. 'I've baffled them, see! One of them arrogant fools said he didn't know why I'd prefer to live among the natives to *earning the wages of honest industry*.' He said the final words mimicking a superior's voice, and then waved his arm in disgust.

'Honest industry, pff! Clearing land that's not theirs – they call that *honest*. I want no part of it.'

Archie's head throbbed. He wished the man would stop talking but Wilson leaned forwards and said in a milder tone, 'Not sure if you was planning on heading over yonder to ask for help.' He nodded towards the settlement again. 'But a word of advice ... If they see you was roaming the forest like a vagrant, they'll label you of the criminal class. And if you're poor ...' he eyed the dirty, oversized jacket hanging off Archie's shoulders, 'you'll be classed as having no morals ... and so a danger.' Wilson winked, and Archie managed a nod as he laid his head back to the ground.

'We'll leave off with your questions now, lad; we must be off. We just wanted to see you right.'

'But ...' Archie was seized with alarm at the thought of being left alone in the dark. He wasn't capable of moving without help, let alone warding off danger.

'Ah, don't fear. We'll shift you to a safe place,' Wilson assured him.

Ballooderry began dividing the yield of their hunt, which included possum and other, smaller, creatures that Archie couldn't make out, as well as the goanna. Wilson draped a large dead python across his shoulders as if to strengthen his wild image. Ballooderry bundled his spears and other equipment, and then smothered the fire as the men spoke together in a language Archie didn't understand.

'I am late,' Wilson said, turning to Archie, 'but the master will excuse me as I'm bringing food to his table.'

They lifted him and carried him downhill to the most northerly point of Tar-Ra, further around the headland from Dawes's hut. They placed him in a concealed position near the waterfront with a view across the wide entrance of Sydney Cove.

'You'll have no fire,' Wilson said, as he bent to place a kangaroo skin over him along with food wrapped in paperbark. He also set a large shell within arm's reach and filled it from his water flask. Seeing fear on Archie's face, he patted the ground before standing. 'You'll be safe here now.'

'I will return by and by,' said Ballooderry. 'Here is easy to come in my nawi.' He waved his hand to indicate Archie's closeness to the water's edge. 'I will come after our corroboree.' He pointed across the water. 'At Bennelong's Point ...'

Archie had a flash of recognition: *Bennelong Point, that's where the Sydney Opera House is built. But how did I know that?*

'Sleep now, lad,' Wilson said, raising a hand as they walked away.

And Archie did, almost instantly.

****

Chapter 23

Voices

Loud laughter jolted Archie out of a timeless sleep. Unaware of what had woken him, he lay with his eyes closed, listening. It seemed strange that he couldn't hear the usual drone of traffic – no sirens, revving engines or screeching brakes ... only the buzzing of insects. *Where am I?*

He blinked his eyes open in a confused state. It was pitch black around him but above the sky was ablaze with stars. He pushed himself onto his elbow and was instantly reminded he'd had some kind of accident – everything hurt with the movement.

'Hello,' he whispered into the darkness. 'Anyone there?'

He should have been afraid, being there alone – who knows where – but somehow he wasn't.

He felt oddly comforted by the memory of someone saying, 'You'll be safe here.' It was the same man who'd left the kangaroo skin and water beside him. He took a drink then slowly twisted and shuffled his body to look in the opposite direction – to the other side of the cove, where he saw several campfires glowing. It sounded like some sort of gathering. Against the firelight he could see figures moving. Then a hush seemed to settle, before indistinct voices became gradually clearer – singing and a clapping sound, wood on wood, to a regular beat.

Progressively, the volume and tempo of the vocals increased and the performers moved faster. Then, building to a crescendo, the routine ended abruptly with a communal shout. Vigorous clapping followed and voices called, 'More, more.' Mingled with the applause Archie could hear good-natured chuckles and the occasional deep belly laugh. Then the chatter and merriment came to a hush as a solo voice – mellow and strong – led the next song, taking the melody from high to low and back. The steady pulsing of clapping sticks began again, and younger voices joined in. Archie squinted, trying to make out details. Against the firelight he could see red military jackets in a semicircle. *Soldiers?* Their arms were moving – clapping in time with the beat – clearly getting into the performance.

Now another voice floated into his mind. He remembered someone saying earlier, 'I will come back after the corroboree.' *That's what it is over there … a corroboree.* Everything else was a blur, but it didn't really matter. He lowered himself onto his back and looked up at the sky. He'd never seen so many stars before. *Someone is coming back for me*, he thought as he drifted off again.

****

Just on sunrise Archie felt the ground shudder as a series of blasts reverberated through the air. At first he thought it was thunder, but it wasn't a rumble – it was a succession of booms. *Fireworks? No, more like explosives!* He felt his heart thumping. *A terrorist attack – a gunman firing into a crowd?* Instinctively, and despite his pain, he'd scrunched his legs up and shrunk against the earth trying to be invisible to the attackers. He put his hands to his ears but the explosions kept on: BOOM … BOOM …

Then, suddenly, there was nothing. He waited, hearing only the hammering inside his chest before he dared to look. There was no crowd, no slumped, bloodied bodies – in fact there was no-one about. He was alone in the bush … still. He turned and peered behind, sensing the explosions had come from that way – from down the harbour. But he saw only an apricot glow rippling across its surface, and a streak of pink and orange above the horizon to the east. *What's happening? What am I doing here?* He tried to focus, but all he could remember was that he'd been hurt … some guys had helped him … they were coming back. He just had to wait.

****

A voice came through a chorus of noisy bird calls, the chatter of lorikeets competing with squawking cockatoos. Someone was saying a familiar word over and over. He wished they'd all shut up and just let him sleep. He heard himself grunt, trying to tell them to go away. Then a hand shook his shoulder.

'Archie.'

'What!' His voice snapped in an aggressive manner. The shadow of two men loomed over him – seemingly familiar – the wild-looking one was a convict he remembered.

'What the ...?' he grumbled, trying to raise his upper body. The light hurt his eyes.

A third voice spoke from behind the others. 'Archie, do you remember me?'

He looked up to see Nanberry, and nodded. His head hurt so he laid it back down.

'He needs more sleep.' It was Nanberry's voice again.

'If we can get him into my nawi, I can take him to Go-Mo-Ra.'

Archie saw this speaker was Ballooderry; the one who'd promised to come back.

Someone else said, 'He'll be safer there with his friends.'

Archie didn't understand the next words, spoken in another language, but sensed they were making plans for him. He closed his eyes wondering, *What friends?*

Ballooderry leaned over him and said, 'Archie. We will help you to my nawi.'

With an immense effort Archie pushed himself up and struggled to his knees. Directly ahead, but some distance from the shore, Archie saw the fishing boat that had carried his attackers the day before. It was heading away down harbour, but he shuddered as images flashed before him. He couldn't quite remember what'd happened, but knew that boat signalled danger. He felt everything sway and slumped back to the ground with a thud.

'No ... no ... I can't ...'

'We can carry you ...' But Archie pushed their hands away.

More discussion followed, then Ballooderry turned to him. 'I have fish to deliver to the officers at Parramatta – then I will come back. Nanberry will stay awhile.'

They moved away and he closed his eyes again in relief. *I just need more sleep* ... He dreamed about his father ... he was waving as he drove away, and calling, *I'll come back for you later.*

****

Chapter 24

Learning Curves

At Go-Mo-Ra, Jemima and Oliver were debating the cause of the early morning blasts that had woken them both, and were baffled that Millie had slept through the din. When she'd finally stirred, Millie wondered whether to tell them about Ann but, as Jemima appeared grumpy, she'd decided to wait.

'Sounded more like missiles to me,' Oliver said, continuing their discussion with a confident air.

'Oh, and you'd know all about that, wouldn't you?' Jemima snapped, feeling edgy and anxious about Archie. They were still arguing the source of the noise when the sight of Boorong approaching from the escarpment froze their conversation. They'd assumed anyone coming to the camp site would arrive by water, given the ruggedness of the terrain from the top of the ridge. Jemima hurried to her feet and met Boorong at the edge of the clearing.

'Have you seen Archie, Boorong?' she blurted without saying hello. She noticed that Boorong's face was decorated with lines of white clay, but was too worried about her brother to comment.

'No, but Ballooderry found him. He will bring him,' Boorong replied.

Jemima's shoulders slumped with relief before she erupted with a stream of questions about Archie's whereabouts and condition.

Boorong lifted her hand to halt Jemima's demands as she strolled past her. 'He will tell you all … when he can.'

Jemima became quiet, wondering what she meant by 'when he can …' but Boorong was already heading to the campfire, where

Oliver and a sleepy-looking Millie greeted her.

Why doesn't she want to talk about Archie? Jemima felt a flood of anxiety but consoled herself that she'd see him soon.

'Was your make-up for the corroboree, Boorong?' Millie asked, but seeing Boorong's brow crease, she rephrased. 'I mean your face decoration – it looks great!' Getting the gist, Boorong beamed, showing brilliant white teeth as she pulled up the sleeve of her frock to reveal further painted-on designs.

'Yes, for our corroboree, but what is *great*?'

'It means *very good* ... And did the officers like your corroboree?'

Boorong reacted with a broad smile again. 'Oh yes! The officers said *boojery caribberie* many times – it means *a good dance*. *Boojery* means *good* – maybe it means the same as *great*?' Boorong's face radiated happiness, recalling the evening's activities. 'Some of the officers tried to dance same as our men – it was very funny – everyone laughing. Captain Hunter said our corroboree was ...' she squinted, trying to recall his exact words, '... well worth seeing ...'

'I reckon it would be ...'

'What was that noise before, Boorong? Like big blasts.' Oliver thrust his arms upwards.

Boorong looked from one to the other, confused by their question. *Have they never heard British cannons before?*

'A gun salute – for Captain Hunter's sailing.' Their blank looks told her nothing. 'You know, when cannons are fired for important people ...'

'Oh yeah, I've seen it on TV ... where we come from, um.' Oliver hesitated, unsure how to explain.

'TV? Yes, tell me about where you come from ...' Boorong directed her gaze at Oliver as she added a small piece of wood to the fire.

Oliver decided to steer the conversation away from TV. 'Well, where we live, everything ... is um ... well, the houses are bigger.'

'As big as the gov'nor's house? With stairs?' Boorong's eyes had widened in fascination.

'Well, yeah. Some buildings have many levels.' Oliver stepped his hand upwards to demonstrate multistorey buildings, then he looked up at the sky, trying to find words to explain skyscrapers. It'd sound ridiculous to say some people lived so high above the ground that their building reached into the clouds. And how could he explain they used elevators? For that matter, how could he explain electricity, air-con, supermarkets, motorways, air travel? Boorong was watching him, waiting for him to continue. He decided to switch to shopping ... at least he could liken it to the provisions store in Sydney.

'You know how people in Sydney Cove get their ration from the public store?'

Boorong nodded.

'Well, where we live, we go somewhere called a *supermarket*. It's really huge – where we can get just about anything we need ... like meat and bread and fruit and ...' He wanted to add *and ice-cream, cake, cookies, soft drink, marshmallows, chocolate, strawberry milk, corn chips, donuts ... etc., etc.,* but knew he couldn't. Instead, he said, 'And we can get stuff – I mean food – at the supermarket anytime.'

'Su-per-mar-ket,' Boorong repeated. 'Like here ...' She waved her hand at the surrounding bush. 'We can get everything we need. See over there.' She pointed to a clump of reedy grass with long strappy leaves. 'See the little flowers ... we soak them for a sweet drink, and when the weather is warmer, we grind its seeds to make our seedcakes. And the low part of its leaves – is good to eat too.'

'I've seen that grass, but I didn't know you could eat it!' Millie went over to inspect.

'Tell me more about where you live,' Boorong said to Oliver.

'About your clothes and ...'

'Why don't you tell Boorong about department stores, Ollie? Tell her what we can buy there ... and how to shop online.' Jemima knew she was being mean but couldn't help herself as she watched Oliver squirm; he was way out of his comfort zone. But Boorong was already thinking about a different topic, triggered by the word *clothes*.

'I forgot to tell you – I met Mary Mullins on my way here. She was at the camp site, where she first met you. She was looking for the clothes she gave you.'

'Oh, I feel bad about those clothes ...' Millie mumbled, '... and about us taking off without a word.'

'She talked about the place you came from. She said it is beyond the mountains?' Boorong directed her question to Jemima, who looked away while deciding how to respond. But Boorong ploughed on. 'She wants to go there – to that place. Is it true you don't have floggings? No-one works in chains?'

'Yes, that's true.' Jemima was relieved she could reply honestly. 'So, you know Mary Mullins?'

'Oh yes, I always saw her at Reverend Johnson's Sunday sermons – and other times. She said, if I see you, to say she wants to go with you ... to see your place.'

'What about her friend – the girl with her when we first met them? We didn't see her again.'

'You mean Ann Harmsworth? She will sail to Norfolk Island soon ... so Mary will lose her friend.'

'Oh, poor Mary – she doesn't have much of a life here, but ...'

'I told her you are still lost, but I didn't tell her about Arch ...' Boorong looked uneasy, but at that moment everyone's attention was caught by a voice calling from the water.

Boorong waved. 'That is my brother, Ballooderry.' Then,

frowning, she added, 'But why is he alone?'

Jemima turned to see the most striking young male she had ever laid eyes on. Wearing only trousers rolled up to his knees, he was dragging his nawi onto the sand. As he approached the campfire she noticed raised ornamental scarrings on his upper chest and across his shoulders.

'Hello,' he smiled at each of them.

She managed a greeting before a rush of anxiety brought her back to earth. 'Archie? Where is he?'

'He will come by and by ... He is sleeping now ...'

At once, Jemima, Oliver and Millie plied him with questions while Boorong sat beside the fire, preparing a meal with ingredients Ballooderry had supplied. He responded tactfully, trying not to raise alarm. He said he would return to check on Archie after a trip to Parramatta and assured them he would bring him to Go-Mo-Ra later. Jemima was still uneasy about her brother, but told herself she had to trust Ballooderry.

As they ate a meal of fish, fresh greens and hard bread brought from the settlement, Jemima and Ballooderry settled into a separate conversation. She was captivated by the deep tone of his voice and the way he pronounced English words.

He told her he lived much of the time at Government House, and that Governor Phillip had invited him to sail to England along with Bennelong when the time came. She saw his delight when he spoke about his trading business with the British officers at Parramatta, supplying them with fresh meat and fish on a regular basis. He nodded towards his newly built nawi, which, he told her, he'd only recently completed. Jemima could see it was his pride and joy.

At his suggestion they walked to the water's edge to examine it up close, and she was captivated as he described, using lots of gestures, the steps involved: the process, he explained, began with choosing the correct timber from the right-sized tree. Then he cut the nawi's outline into the tree trunk so that one single piece of bark could later be carefully removed using stone hatchets and wooden mallets. Wedges, he explained, were left in place until, over time, the bark loosened from the tree to just the right degree, when it was skilfully removed, made pliable with fire and gradually formed into the correct shape. Then the ends were pleated and tightly bound. 'Like this,' Ballooderry pointed to thick fibre at each end of his nawi.

'Wow, I've never seen anything handmade like this before. It's unreal.' And she meant it.

'Never seen handmade ...? How can I build without my hands?' He was baffled but thrilled with her admiration. 'And what is *unreal*?' His eyes shone with laughter.

'It means *very good*.' Jemima beamed back at him. 'Like *boojery* – this is boojery nawi.' She spread her hands towards the vessel and they blushed and laughed again.

Then, after a brief pause, Ballooderry said, 'I must go to Parramatta now, but I will return later with Archie.' They walked back to the fireside, where the others sat watching them approach with amused expressions. Ballooderry picked up his net bag, slung it over his shoulder and said his goodbyes.

As Jemima waved him off, she felt a warm confidence that their next meeting would bring Archie, as well as more happy conversation. Little did she know that this would not be the case.

****

Chapter 25

Millie

Settling back at the fireside a little apart from the others, Jemima thought about Ballooderry's return. She ran her fingers through her hair, wondering what she looked like.

'Geez, I'd love to clean up. Does anyone want to go for a swim? The water looks *so* inviting.'

When no-one replied she turned to see the others absorbed in their own conversation. Boorong was speaking in a low serious tone; Millie and Oliver were listening attentively.

'When I'm in Sydney Cove, I see some of the white people thinking they are better, more important ... I asked Mr Dawes the meaning of *primitive* and *savage* that I hear them say when I go past. And I see the way they watch my people.' Boorong tilted her chin upwards and looked down her nose, with a pose suggesting assumed power and superiority. She was such a good mimic, and her impersonation was so convincing that the serious mood was broken and laughter broke loose.

'Yes, yes; it's the same where we come from ...' Millie was giggling and nodding vigorously.

Jemima now felt compelled to join the conversation, and tapped Boorong on the arm.

'My grandma – my mother's mother – comes from the south coast. She met Grandpa – he's Greek – when he came from Greece to work on the Snowy Mountains Scheme. My grandma – she's a proud Koori ...' Boorong didn't understand all of Jemima's words but picked up on the last one.

Koori?'

'Yeah, it means *people* – same as you. Koori people live all along this coast, still ... now ...' Jemima waved her hand to indicate to the north and south. 'I want to find out more about Grandma now.' Then she placed her arm next to Millie's. 'See, my skin's darker ... not as white as Millie's. She's got Irish ...'

'Yes, I see ... but some of my people are like you – their skin is lighter – not all the same.' Boorong paused, looking thoughtful. 'We have different meanings for *white*.' She picked up a small, brilliant white shell, radiant in the sunlight, and held it against Millie's pale skin. 'No person is white like this shell ...' She chuckled at the idea. 'The English word *white* means like this shell – and like my white clay.' She ran her finger along the stark white lines highlighted against her dark skin. 'We call this *ta-boa* – white.

'But ...' She opened the palm of her hand and placed it beside Millie's arm. 'When we speak of *white skin*, our meaning is like this.' She held both palms up to show their pale skin tone.

'Wow, that's cool.' Millie was staring at her own palms. 'Cos no-one's actually *white* or *black*. We're all somewhere in between.'

'Come on, that's enough philosophy for today; let's go for a swim?' Jemima cut in, as she stood and headed for the water. As she let its coolness wash over her feet, it struck her how clean the water was; there was no floating scum, no plastic wrappers, broken bottles or lids. She could see her brightly painted toenails through the water as if it was glass.

'Okay,' Millie said, joining her. 'But then I want Boorong to show us how to make a sweet drink from those wildflowers.'

They had all reached the water's edge when Boorong said, 'After this I must go. I want to see my little sister, Milbah. I love to make her laugh and she begins to say words now ...' She paused because they had all turned to her with open mouths.

Boorong couldn't fathom their reaction, but continued, 'Milbah is Mrs Johnson's baby. She is not my *real* sister, but I was there when she was born and I asked Mrs Johnson to give her that name.'

'That is *my* real name,' said Millie. 'But I've never, ever heard anyone else called Milbah before!' She felt a strange sensation, as she had done in the tunnel when she'd seen initials carved in the sandstone walls, and when she'd first heard Mary Mullins's name.

'Milbah is girl's name among my people and Mrs Johnson liked it, and I think she wants to please me.'

'Wow,' was all Millie said, but inwardly she felt engrossed with the thought that two names linked her to this time and place – first Mary Mullins and now Milbah. And Ann Smith had singled her out to share her story. *Why was that?* It played on her mind.

****

After Boorong left, they spent some time exploring along the water's edge and collecting firewood.

Looking from the water back at the steeply sloping wooded hillside, Millie noticed a number of large rock overhangs with cleared areas in front of them – similar to their first camping spot. She pointed them out to the others.

'Why are all those camps empty? We see the local people paddling their nawis across the harbour, but why aren't they camped around here?'

'Maybe cos a lot of them didn't survive smallpox,' Oliver suggested. 'Remember what you read in that journal you found? Or maybe most of them are staying in Sydney Cove now.'

'But surely they'd rather be here,' Millie said as she watched a flock of excited lorikeets descend on a nearby tree. She startled herself, voicing such a thought, and looked up to meet her brother's amused expression, which said, *You've changed!*

Throughout the afternoon, they peered across the water in anticipation of Ballooderry's arrival with Archie, but saw only nawis passing in the distance. Several times Jemima raised the question of how long it might take to paddle to Parramatta and back, and repeatedly mumbled, 'They should be here by now.'

On their way back to the camp, Millie brought up Boorong's unexpected message from Mary Mullins. 'Imagine Mary in *our* Sydney – trying to take it all in, trying to make sense of it.'

'It'd be like entering another dimension.' Oliver thought this could be the moment to bring up his time-travel theory. But Jemima immediately cut him off.

'Don't start, Ollie – I'm not in the mood for a sci-fi rant. Let's just enjoy the peace.'

Millie saw her brother's resentment about to burst, so tried to move the conversation along. 'Yeah, it'd be hard for her to adjust to the noise – the sirens and jackhammers and traffic speeding past her. Imagine her seeing helicopters and planes and drones for the first time.'

'Do you reckon she'd notice the air's different? I guess she'd have to, really – no fumes here.'

'And imagine her watching TV for the first time, and us trying to explain it – or a phone or laptop for that matter – or trying to get her into an elevator.'

'Yeah, but overall her life'd be easier in our time. I mean, we've got washing machines and dishwashers ...'

'She said she liked cleaning, though. I think there'd be some pluses to a simpler life ... there's more time to just – I don't know, to just *be*.'

'Except she hasn't got much choice here – especially when it comes to a partner – only stinky convicts to choose from.' They all made exaggerated groaning sounds at the thought of Mary's options.

****

Returning to the camp site with armfuls of wood, Jemima rekindled the fire. Oliver found wattle leaves to put in the rock pool in the hope of catching fish as Nanberry had done. Millie gathered some edible greens that Boorong had pointed out on the edge of the clearing. But, as the afternoon wore on, Jemima spent most of the time gazing expectantly into the distance.

'At least we know Archie's with either Nanberry or Ballooderry,'

Millie said, trying to keep the concern from her voice. But by the time the sun began slipping behind the mountains they were all extremely worried. Ballooderry had not returned as promised.

****

Chapter 26

Choices

Hours had passed with Nanberry sitting, quietly sharpening stone wedges on the rock shelf, when Archie finally stirred and raised himself onto his elbow.

'The ship's gone,' he said, looking towards the cove. 'And my head feels ... clearer.'

'Yes, Captain Hunter left before sunrise – to sail to England.' Nanberry was happy to finally chat, especially about ships. 'I want to sail in a ship one day and go far away and ... *explore*. Ballooderry and Bennelong will sail to England with the gov'nor when he leaves here.'

'Mm.' Archie wasn't ready for conversation but shuffled himself into a seated position and reached for the water. His memory was returning in brief flashes but he was still disorientated. He looked around and remembered being carried in the darkness to this place. Now that it was light, he saw Bennelong's brick house on the opposite headland of the cove – *there'd been dancing and laughter over there.*

He looked in the other direction, towards the steep ridge, and immediately a frightening image flickered through his mind – *Jemima and Millie are disappearing over the crest.*

And he is running ... struggling to catch up with them ... being chased ... and some men grab him from behind ... They'd all been running earlier, too – from the barracks where they'd watched a flogging.

The bloody scene jolted Archie's memory. They are all here ... hiding in Sydney Cove ... because they'd gone back in time ... somehow. With a surge of urgency he turned to Nanberry.

'Jemima! My sister ... where is my sister? And Millie ... and

144

Oliver?' He was trying to get to his feet.

Nanberry put out his hand to still him. 'Don't move too fast, Archie. They are safe. Do not fret.'

Archie was on his knees and nodded weakly. The rush of adrenaline had sapped his energy.

'Can we go see them, Nanberry? I'll need … your help … My legs feel cramped but I need to get moving.' Archie knew now that he couldn't walk without Nanberry's help. 'I'll get this off first … it's too heavy,' he said, pulling his arms out of Mr Peat's coat.

'You must slow down, Archie, and you must wait here. Ballooderry will be here soon to take you in his nawi. He has been away a long time already … I must go presently, but I will wait with you a little longer. I must visit Mr Dawes on my way back,' Nanberry said, looking in the direction of the observatory.

'Is it safe for me here in the daylight?' Archie scanned all directions now that he remembered why he must stay concealed.

'There's no reason for anyone to come this way, and now that it is late afternoon, the convicts are restricted to the main settlement … unless they have permission to hunt. Look, I brought you some bread from the bakery.'

Archie saw it was the same hard stuff he'd had before, but smiled and took a bite.

'You like Mr Dawes, don't you?'

'Yes … it is his wish to stay here. I think the men who sailed today – they were pleased to leave. And most white people here – they want to go to their country, England. But Mr Dawes …' Nanberry nodded in the direction of Dawes's observatory. 'He says he's found a different life here – he wants to learn from my people – and this place. He wants to stay, but the gov'nor won't give him permission till he apologises for speaking against the gov'nor's actions.'

'What actions?' Archie's curiosity sparked.

'Well, the gov'nor sent soldiers southwards to punish some of my people for spearing a very bad white man. Mr Dawes was ordered to go on that expedition, and he obeyed, though he didn't want to.' Nanberry looked directly into Archie's face before continuing. 'But when they reached Botany Bay they didn't find anyone – there was no-one there – because I sent word that soldiers were coming.'

'*You* did?'

'They think I don't understand the talk at the gov'nor's house because I am just a boy – and sometimes it is not easy to know what I should do.'

Archie nodded; he could certainly relate to that.

'When Mr Dawes returned to Sydney after that expedition, he told the gov'nor he would never obey such an order again.'

'And did he apologise when the governor demanded it?'

'No, he refused – he said he would *not betray his conscience.* So I will be sad when Mr Dawes sails away ... *You* saw how he listens to us at Tar-Ra – it is our place for laughing and sharing.'

'Yes.' The conversation had distracted Archie but now he stretched and tried to stand again. 'I think I need to move a bit now.'

'You *must* stay hidden, Archie – just walk back and forth behind these bushes ...'

After a while Nanberry said, 'When I came here – to Sydney Cove – I was very sick and I thought all my people were dead from smallpox. Later, I saw some are still alive like me. Surgeon White saved me, you know ...'

Archie nodded.

'He is a good man, but it is not the same as living with ... my people.'

'Yes, I understand,' said Archie. 'I don't live with *my* father. He lives a long way from me – on a farm in the Snowy Mountains but, when we find our way home, I'm going to visit him. I've made up my mind.'

Nanberry looked thoughtful. 'Surgeon White told me he will return to England one day – I will be sad when he sails. Then I will live with my people again and I will become a warrior. You see, we have a special tooth ceremony for that.' Nanberry gestured as if to pull out his upper right front tooth. 'We have a name for that but you won't know it … Then I will be a man, a brave Gadigal warrior.'

Archie, feeling a little brighter, felt the urge for friendly banter. 'So you're going to be a Gadigal warrior *and* a sailor with the British?'

'Yes, I am,' Nanberry smiled back, but the passion in his eyes told Archie he was deadly serious.

'Archie, I must go now; Mr White is expecting me. Come, I will see you are settled and well hidden. Ballooderry will be here soon – he is *never* this late returning from Parramatta …' Then, out of the blue, and with an abrupt shove, Nanberry's voice became urgent. 'Quick – get down!'

Archie fell with a thud and a groan.

'It's the Lump … stay down. It takes goods to and from Parramatta along the river.'

Archie peered through the bushes to see what looked like a large raft or barge moving slowly, from the west, into Sydney Cove. It was piled with sacks and boxes, as well as passengers and crew.

'Get back to your hiding spot, Archie, and stay there. Don't move. I must go enquire about Ballooderry.' And he was gone.

****

Chapter 27

Dead End

At Go-Mo-Ra, Jemima's emotions were in turmoil. She paced back and forth across the clearing before plonking herself between her cousins.

'Well, we can't sit here doing nothing. This is serious, and Ballooderry has completely let us down.' *He seemed so … genuine and kind and open,* she thought, *but his actions show otherwise.*

To the west, the sun was setting in a spectacular display of crimson and purple streaks, but it went completely unnoticed. Millie and Oliver were watching Jemima's agitation grow and were feeling increasingly unsettled too.

'We're stranded here, and … and at the mercy of virtual strangers.' Jemima was ranting again. 'Yes, I know Nanberry and Boorong have been more than helpful. But where are they now, when we need them most? It'll be dark soon!' *Where* are *they?* She threw her arms up in despair. 'We can't just sit here. Something's happened – something is going on!'

'Okay,' Millie ventured. 'Why don't we follow the shoreline around towards Dawes Point – I mean, Tar-Ra – before it starts getting too dark? We know Archie's there.'

Jemima huffed as if to say, *Do we?*

'There's a track over there …' Millie gestured to the left of the camp site. 'It follows the shoreline.'

'How do you know?'

'Cos I went for a walk last night after you went to sleep …' Jemima looked at her as if she'd gone out of her mind, so Millie decided to leave it at that.

'So you're saying, if we keep following it, eventually we'd have to arrive at Tar-Ra? But we've all got sore feet – is it a good idea?'

Oliver posed the questions, peering towards the edge of the clearing where Millie had indicated.

'We can soak our feet if we need to – the track stays close to the water. Come on,' Millie stood and headed to the spot where she remembered following Ann Smith into the forest.

Oliver tailed her with Jemima shadowing them without further objection.

Millie ducked under the bushes and picked out the narrow trail leading through the forest. The path was not well defined – sections were concealed by long grass and sprawling bushes – so she knew it would be easy to lose their way. She couldn't remember how far it was to the little beach where she'd swum, but knew to keep the water to her left. The shadows were becoming longer, and she had to watch for low overhanging branches and warn the others when to stoop as they followed her cautiously. She was beginning to wonder why Jemima wasn't complaining when something smacked against her cheek, then spread across her face. She stopped dead. 'Argh!'

Realising instantly what it was, she began frantically brushing the thick spider's web out of her hair and off her shoulders. 'Argh! Get it off me! Can you see a spider on me anywhere, Ollie? Quick, check – the back of my head – quick, Ollie! Quick!'

Oliver had bumped into her when she'd stopped suddenly, but now he was trying not to laugh.

'Oh, Mil – let me have a look – turn around,' he said as he flicked and brushed her head, back and shoulders. 'Nothing there,' he said flippantly. 'I was just thinking how brave you've been. Here, grab a stick and wave it in front of you, cos now's the time of day spiders are building their webs.'

'No, you go first from now on,' she said, pushing her brother in front. 'We're nearly at the little beach I remember. And if we keep going past that – following the shoreline – we have to end up at Tar-Ra.'

'And what then?' It was the first time Jemima had spoken since they'd left the camp site. 'I know doing *something* is better than doing nothing ... but we don't know exactly where Archie is, do we? Or how long it'll take us to get there – or what to do *when* we get there.'

Millie ignored her as she searched ahead for the side track that led to the swimming spot.

'Okay, there's the beach I saw when I came along here last night. This is the furthest I came, so let's hope this track continues all the way around the headland.'

With Oliver in the lead, they passed the strip of sand where Millie had sat with Ann and Dingo, and made their way around a bend in the track with a raised bank to their right. The terrain ahead was changing – becoming more exposed to the wind. They were approaching a wide, flat outcrop of rocks reaching into the harbour, when they were brought to an abrupt halt at the sight of a towering figure staring down at them from the side of the track. There was enough twilight to see a fierce, dark face examining them with intense scrutiny.

Oliver was closest and didn't know whether to shrink to his knees or run for his life. The man had clearly been waiting for them. He stood very still, silently watching them with piercing eyes ... His appearance was made striking by the bone he wore pierced through the cartilage of his nose. He was tall and broad shouldered – the embodiment of a warrior. He wore a kangaroo skin draped from his waist and had feathers and other decorations in his hair. His upper body was scarred in a similar manner to Ballooderry's, and he was holding a spear in one hand – not poised as if to hurl it – but with it pointing skywards. Oliver imagined that could change in an instant though – they could all be pierced through before they could blink. As the man surveyed them, Oliver was sure they were in deadly danger. *Things could become lethal very quickly*, he told himself.

The warrior's presence was imposing and powerful. No-one moved or spoke until he did. After what seemed like a long wait, he pointed at the rocks ahead and their eyes followed his signal.

'This is wrong …' His voice boomed, deep and gruff, but his English was clear. They instinctively took a step back.

'Sorry,' Jemima exclaimed. 'We don't mean to do wrong … we're lost.' She held her hands out in appeal. 'We are trying to find my brother.' Her voice quivered but she stood her ground, trying not to show her terror.

The man made a sound like *mm* in his throat and pointed along the track the way they had come. 'You must go –'

Oliver didn't wait for him to finish, but blurted a response on behalf of them all. 'Yes, yes; we are going,' he said as they continued to reverse away from him.

We've just got to get away before he gets more agitated, Jemima thought in panic.

The man looked impatient when he repeated himself, and then completed his words cut off by Oliver.

'You must go … that way home.' He was pointing behind them. the way they had come.

'What?'

'That way …' he nodded abruptly. 'That way home,' he said again with slow deliberate words.

'Home?'

'Yes …' He pointed towards the rocks ahead. 'That way … is wrong way.'

He stepped down onto the track in front of them and then onto the rock shelf just ahead. They watched him, with the point of his spear, chip off a piece of oyster shell and hold it out to show them.

'Wrong,' he motioned in the direction of the route they'd been planning to take.

'Oh? We shouldn't go that way?'

He nodded gruffly and gestured at the sharp oyster shells that they could now see covered the whole area. Then he pointed to their feet.

'Oh yes, we see now – the oyster shells will cut our feet.'

He nodded, and then pointed again the way they had come.

'That is your way … home.'

He indicated that they should ascend the slope at an angle, then change direction somehow and backtrack down the slope. They watched his gestures without getting his meaning. They just wanted to get away.

'I know you want to leave this place.'

'Oh, thank you – yes, yes we do. But we have to find my brother first … we don't know what's happened to him.'

'You will find him …' There was a long pause – so long that they thought he had finished his message and they should leave, but then the man tilted his head and said, 'I wish you well …'

After a moment's hesitation – as if he was debating whether to say more – he took a step up onto the bank, dipped his head again and melted into the forest.

They looked at each other and, without a word, it was agreed they should head back to the camp site without delay.

****

Chapter 28

Tar-Ra

Twilight was creeping across the harbour in purple hues when Archie saw Nanberry approaching, breathless and agitated. His head was bent and his shoulders hunched. Archie hadn't seen him like that before.

'I have risked much trouble returning here,' he said in a rush, '... to tell you that Ballooderry won't be coming in his nawi to take you anywhere!' His voice held a bitterness which was at odds with his usual easy-going nature.

'Um, Why?' Archie hardly dared to ask. Nanberry's harshness had him feeling that whatever had happened to Ballooderry was his fault.

'His nawi has been smashed to pieces!'

Archie could see that Nanberry was fighting tears of anger or frustration.

'It was completely destroyed by some evil convicts ... venting their jealousy at his ... success.' Nanberry flopped down next to Archie, who looked around as if the evidence may be somewhere within view.

Nanberry took a deep breath before launching into the details. 'It happened at Parramatta – I heard about it at the wharf while the Lump was being unloaded. I waited because it's where I hear much news. Ballooderry left his nawi a short distance from the settlement while he took fish to the officers' huts. When he got back he saw it broken into many ... totally destroyed.'

'I don't know what to say, Nanberry ...'

'People said he stared in disbelief at first, but then he was overtaken by anger. When they described the men who did it, he swore his revenge and went in a rage to the gov'nor's headquarters at Parramatta to report it, saying he will find them and punish them himself.'

Nanberry had sat with his head bowed while retelling the story so far, but now he looked at Archie. 'But, Archie, I think you already know the British think their justice is superior.'

Archie nodded silently.

'While I was at the wharf, I heard Judge Collins telling Mr Tench what happened. He said Ballooderry was in a terrible state when he saw the gov'nor, who happened to be at Parramatta today. He said Ballooderry's face, arms and chest were painted with red clay – it is a sign of his great anger – and that he waved his spears while vowing to punish the men who smashed his canoe.'

'Mr Collins said the gov'nor made Ballooderry promise he would not take his own revenge,' Nanberry paused and let out a long sigh, ... 'which Ballooderry agreed to because the gov'nor said *he* would hang those that destroyed Ballooderry's nawi.'

Nanberry looked away and then back at Archie, before he continued. 'Then I saw Judge Collins lower his voice and say, "But of course, that was only to satisfy the lad at the time."'

'You see, Archie, the gov'nor does not understand the ways of my people – that it belongs to Ballooderry to punish the wrong against him. When he learns he was fed a lie, he will seek his own way to settle this with those convicts. And then there will be big trouble – the gov'nor will send soldiers to seize him and he will be punished in the British way for injuring a white man.'

'I am very sad about this, Archie. The officers always say Ballooderry is *a fine young man* – I know the gov'nor thinks so. He invited him to sail to England. But I think it will all go wrong now ...'

Listening to Nanberry's story, Archie became increasingly anxious; he didn't know what to say. He felt for Nanberry and Ballooderry but he was also very worried about his own precarious situation.

'So what will happen ..?'

'Boorong, she is Ballooderry's sister – she was at the wharf with Mrs Johnson. She also heard what happened today. We talked about you and she said she will take you to Go-Mo-Ra – it will be before sunrise.'

****

Chapter 29

Night Visitors

After Nanberry left, it had taken Archie a very long time to get to sleep. When he woke in the darkness, he lay thinking over and over about Ballooderry's plight. And worse, the injustice that Nanberry thought would now follow.

He was tossing restlessly, trying to get comfortable and thinking about his father, when something – he didn't know what – made him freeze. It wasn't a sound; it was a feeling. He lay absolutely still and tried to gauge why and where the feeling had come from. It was a movement on the water he'd sensed – just the slightest breath of a movement – a drifting. It was too dark to see anything.

Can it be Ballooderry, returning in a borrowed nawi? He didn't risk lifting his head to check. Whatever it was, it had seemed bigger than a nawi as it had passed by. He tried to steal a look but the night was pitch black against the water and it was impossible to decipher anything.

Then on his opposite side, where thick bushes concealed him, he heard a different movement. It seemed as if someone – or something – was creeping slowly towards him. He dared not breathe. Maybe there was more than one. A twig snapped, followed by a deep throaty growl. Whoever, or whatever, it was, it was getting closer. Archie flattened himself against the ground and willed himself not to move or make a sound. When he heard a barely audible voice whisper, 'This way,' he felt a wave of relief, thinking it must be lovers looking for a secluded spot. But he realised that was unlikely so far from the main settlement.

The next sound was a muffled squeal, like someone was crying with a hand over their mouth.

Oh hell, he thought. *What now?* He pulled Mr Peat's coat over his head, leaving just an ear exposed so he could keep track of the movement. Whoever it was had passed by now and was nearer the water – then *in* the water, wading out from the shore. He slowly twisted his body to face the cove and stole a peek. He could make out what seemed like a huge bulk sitting close to the shore. Its mass was outlined against a star-filled sky. He squinted, trying to adjust his eyes, to make out its size. He heard a plop like an anchor being dropped.

It had to be a boat – but why here, in the middle of the night?

Someone else was approaching now, ever so slowly, from the bush, along the same rough track. It sounded like more than one person and as if they were dragging something heavy. It seemed pretty obvious to Archie now why they'd chosen the middle of the night. And he didn't want to think about what they'd do to him if they discovered him lying there, witnessing their mischief.

'Can you see the bloody boat?' The husky male voice was instantly familiar – the way it stretched out the word *boat* to sound like *bought*. He remembered that voice saying, *We'll take him to the boat. Throw him to the sharks.*

It came from almost above or beside him – only one clump of bushes screened his prone body. He wanted to roll himself further under its foliage but he didn't dare move a muscle. They were so close he could have reached under the bushes and grabbed their ankles. He was shaking uncontrollably now.

'Shut up and just keep going.' The whispered response sounded edgy and threatening.

Archie didn't think he could feel more terrified, and for the second time in two days he thought, *This is it. I'm dead meat.*

But their bulky frames passed, huffing and puffing with the load they were lugging. Archie allowed himself to relax enough to slide himself further into the undergrowth. Then, with his side pushed against the trunk, he listened for a hint of what may happen next. He heard the men reach the waterside and pause to rearrange the weight to carry it across the water to the boat.

The next sound stunned him. It was a woman's voice, softly hushing an infant as she approached from the same direction that the others had come from. The child was whimpering as the woman struggled along.

'Shush now, Charlotte. Don't wriggle; you're heavy for Mama.'

The woman paused so close to Archie he could hear her raspy breath. It was more than the panting of exertion – she was breathless with fear. He could smell the sweat of her terror.

'Quiet now. We're all goin' in the gov'nor's boat. Your wee brother's already there. Be still.' Her voice was a trembly whisper.

Gov'nor's boat? The stifled cry he'd heard before must've come from the baby brother.

The woman readjusted the bundle, but the child continued to squirm, and she almost stumbled into the bushes that hid Archie. But she staggered on towards the cove, where there was the slightest swish of water against the boat's timbers.

He heard muted instructions coming from the cove, before a rustle from the track caught his attention again. More footsteps. Heavier than those that had already passed. This time there were at least four, maybe even five, sets of feet. And they were carrying hefty loads. A thud, followed by curses, told Archie someone had dropped something.

Feet hurried back from the water's edge. 'What the hell ...?' The man muttered curses to himself as he rushed past Archie to investigate.

'We've dropped stuff, Will, but can't see ... I think a handsaw and scales, and the sack of flour split further back ...'

'Shut up!' The man they'd called Will hissed in frustration. 'Just get to the boat. Leave it, whatever it is,' he murmured tensely. As he herded them from behind, Archie heard him mumbling under his breath, 'I'd be leaving *you*, if I could manage ...'

His voice faded with his retreat to the water and all went quiet, but for the movement of water as they waded through it, and the muffled thumps of sacks and bundles being stowed in the boat. Archie watched its shape rise and dip on the waves as they prepared to up anchor. Eventually, oars came out and the bulk began to move silently down the harbour towards the heads where, Archie guessed, they'd row quietly past the guards on the headland and into the vast Pacific.

An escape! That's what the drama was all about … It's why they'd been chased after seeing those men hide stuff. It must've all been so carefully planned. They must've been stashing food and equipment for months. And they'd chosen a moonless night to make their move. They'd waited till the only ship in the harbour had sailed, earlier that day. And the man called Will, the boss, must have chosen his accomplices for their seafaring skills.

But the size of the vessel! It was only a six-oared fishing boat – belonging to the governor, so someone had said. And there must have been at least ten of them squashed into it, including a woman and two babies. Archie shook his head. He didn't know where they were planning to go once outside the heads but, in any direction, it was the Pacific Ocean!

My ordeal is nothing compared to what theirs will be, he thought, pulling Mr Peat's coat aside to stretch his legs. *As soon as we find that tunnel, we'll have all the comforts of home.*

****

Chapter 30

Me-Mel

Just as the sun was peeping above the cove, Archie saw two nawis approach, their forms silhouetted against the golden backdrop of daybreak. Assuming his visitors were Nanberry and a companion, he shuffled himself into a seated position in readiness for leaving his hiding spot. As the vessels neared the rocks, the occupants steered skilfully to a thin crescent of sand, then pulled their nawis onto the beach and hurried up to him. He now remembered Nanberry said Boorong would come.

'Hello.' She smiled warmly. 'I am Ballooderry's sister. I am Boorong.'

'I'm really sorry about Ballooderry's nawi, Boorong.'

'Yes,' she said. 'It is bad ...' Her reply fell away as she helped Nanberry get Archie to his feet. She bent to pick up the kangaroo skin and remove any evidence that Archie had been hiding there.

'Come, Archie,' Nanberry said hurriedly. 'We need to get away from here before the day begins. Soldiers are already about – something has happened. Put your coat around you and we'll help you into the nawi.'

Archie thought he could manage by himself this time, but he let them support him. He desperately wanted to ask about his sister and the others, and to tell them what he'd witnessed, but they were rushing him to the water's edge. Once he was settled in Boorong's nawi they headed across the harbour, rather than following the rocky shoreline to their west.

'We will take you to *Me-Mel* – it will be safer,' Nanberry called from his vessel. 'Someone has alerted the gov'nor to an escape and his boat is missing, so soldiers will be everywhere soon.'

'Yes,' Archie said in a rush. 'I was there – I saw it!'

Nanberry exchanged a look with Boorong before they both bent forwards, putting their energy into paddling against the tide, heading to an island that sat in the middle of the harbour. Questions and stories would have to wait.

Archie was surprised how fast they were moving through the water as he tried to identify landmarks. *We're heading north-west from Dawes Point,* Archie thought. *No, not Dawes Point – it is called Tar-Ra,* he corrected himself. He then turned around, to look at the headland where he'd lain hidden. He faced forwards again, realising, yes, *Goat Island, that's where we're going.*

They skirted the island and eased into a little cove on its western side, and pulled their nawis into a spot out of sight from the Sydney settlement.

'This place is Me-Mel. It belongs to Bennelong,' Nanberry explained. 'He comes here with his wife Barangaroo when they are not staying at the gov'nor's. But he said you can stay here. He knows you will leave soon.'

They helped Archie up the beach and settled him on a log. He noticed that the camp site was well used and that someone had recently indulged in a shellfish and oyster feast. The morning was still chilly and Archie pulled Mr Peat's coat around his shoulders again.

'Where is my sister, and ...?' Archie paused because Nanberry and Boorong were already hurrying back to the nawis.

When Nanberry returned holding the end of a long smouldering firestick, he said, 'We will go now and bring them all here.'

Boorong had fetched water and food packages from her nawi while Nanberry placed firewood atop dry leaves and kindling in the fireplace, before igniting it with his firestick. After hasty instructions about keeping the fire alight with wood piled beside Archie and advice on how to bake the yams that Boorong had thrown into the coals, they left. Archie watched the nawis disappear, and sat alone once more.

He contented himself with staring into the flames and gazing at the crimson-lit sunlight playing on the water and the foliage cascading down the opposite shore. *I'd never do this in my normal life*, he thought, recognising how the past few days had changed him. He smiled to himself, feeling a surge of gratitude – he couldn't find a word for what – but he felt more alive than he had in a long time. He could feel his physical strength returning too – though not enough to walk to the water's edge alone. He took a deep breath and felt a slight twinge from his ribcage. He breathed again. It felt good to just breathe.

It seemed only a short time later that two nawis came into view from around the bend. He stood and waved both hands above his head at the sight of his sister and cousins. When Jemima reached him she threw her arms around him like she'd never done before. He stifled a groan as she squeezed his injured body.

'Thank goodness you're alive, Archie. I thought I'd lost you.' Then she held him at arm's length and inspected his bruised neck and face, shaking her head, while the others looked on smiling, waiting for their turn to express their relief at seeing him safe.

'Bruises heal,' he said, grinning and enjoying the attention.

With their reunion done, they all sat around the fire enjoying freshly cooked fish and baked yams. Nanberry and Boorong made it clear they weren't staying long, but were keen to hear details of the escape before they left.

'There were at least ten of them,' Archie began, '... including a woman and two little ones.'

'It *was* Mr Bryant, then!' Boorong said, looking at Nanberry. 'And his wife Mary, and little Charlotte and baby Emanuel.'

'Someone brought the boat around to the point – I suppose it was the one they called Will – and the others came by foot to meet it. Lugging and dragging stuff, they were. They dropped some gear, though, so the soldiers will find it and piece it all together – how they did it.' Archie was enjoying being the storyteller.

'I am sad that Will and Mary Bryant are gone,' Boorong said.

'Mr Bryant was chief fisherman', Boorong continued, 'and important to the gov'nor, but many times he said he wanted to go home – to live in his own country. We went fishing with him sometimes – helped pull in the nets. But some of the convict men who worked with him, they were not good men.'

No, they weren't, thought Archie. He saw the others' grim expressions and knew they were thinking the same. 'I've got *so* much more to tell you,' Archie said, remembering Wilson, the corroboree and the explosions. 'But I want to hear what's been happening with you lot.'

Boorong nodded, and stood to leave. 'I will go now. You have much to talk about and I want to visit Mrs Johnson and Milbah again today, but I will come later.'

'Thank you, Boorong. I hope you will have news of what's happened with Ballooderry,' Jemima spoke, but the others nodded. They'd been shocked to hear about Ballooderry's terrible experience when Boorong and Nanberry had brought them up to date.

Nanberry stood up now too, saying he must return his friend's nawi, and they all walked down to the beach together with Jemima, Millie and Oliver helping and fussing over Archie.

'You will have more freedom here, till Archie can travel, because everyone knows this is Bennelong's place,' Nanberry explained. 'But remember: the Lump goes past this island, so be on the watch and stay hidden.'

As they returned to the fireside, Archie explained the Lump was a barge that transported goods and passengers between Sydney and Parramatta.

Oliver was ahead of them and announced he was going to collect firewood and explore around-about. Seeing Millie frown, he assured her his ankle was healing, and he was barely limping anymore.

'Wait, Ollie; I think, whatever we do, we *have* to stay together from now on.' Jemima took a deep breath and continued. 'It's my fault we separated and got into the awful mess we did back there,' she said, flicking her head in the direction of Sydney. 'And I'd never forgive myself if I'd lost you, Archie.'

'Are you actually apologising, Jem?' Oliver said with a twisted smile. 'That'd be a first.'

And they all laughed, including Jemima.

My sister has changed too, thought Archie.

****

Chapter 31

Revelations

With Archie resting by the campfire, the others spent the morning exchanging stories, gathering firewood and exploring nearby, but always within sight of each other. Later, when they were sitting together again, Archie told them about the corroboree he'd seen and heard at Bennelong Point, and how the soldiers had clapped and called out, *Boo-je-ry ca-rib-ber-ie* – a *good dance*.

'Boo-je-ry ca-rib-ber-ie,' the croaky words came from behind.

They spun around in alarm, but there was no-one there. The hoarse, raspy words came again, and they realised they were from an overhanging branch where a cockatoo began prancing along its length, and twisting its head at different angles, as if trying to work out what they were.

'Boo-je-ry ca-rib-ber-ie,' it repeated, followed by, 'Good dance. Good dance.'

'Wow, a bilingual cockatoo,' said Archie, laughing up at the bird as it looked back at him. 'Hello, Cocky,' Archie said, addressing the bird directly. In response the cockatoo raised its yellow crest, fluffed out its feathers and jumped along the limb in an excited fashion. 'You're showing off. Aren't you, mate?'

The bird gave an ear-piercing screech as it flew off to join several others that appeared to be playing a game of tag between distant treetops. The scene had them all smiling as they watched the birds frolicking.

'Yeah, Boorong talked about the corroboree too,' Oliver said, returning to Archie's description. 'She was decorated in white clay for it.'

'And I heard it, when you were both asleep,' Millie addressed Jemima and Oliver in a rush. She thought this might be a good time

165

to tell them about Ann Smith's visit, but Oliver interrupted their conversation by announcing he was going to climb the small bluff behind them to see if he could see across to Barangaroo Reserve.

'I won't go out of sight,' he assured them and took off.

They watched him climb the hill and shade his eyes to look across the water.

When he returned, he announced there was a good view of the western slope of The Rocks area from the ridge. Their conversation turned to finding and planning their way home, as soon as Archie was up to walking. They were feeling relaxed – they were back together again, and it seemed their days in this bizarre situation would soon be over. Millie steered their conversation back to the experiences they'd had.

'I've been thinking,' she announced, looking from one to the other. 'Because this has been the strangest few days of my life, I'm going to write about it – jot notes, anyway. I should've started earlier but it's never too late, they say.' She pulled Tench's quill from her pocket and held it up.

Jemima looked at her as if to say, *you'll need more than that.*

'Just listen for a minute, Jem! I should've asked Nanberry or Boorong if they could get me paper and ink, but it's too late for *that* now so I have a plan. I'm going to try making ink from this soot ... It could work!' she said in response to her cousins' sceptical expressions.

Millie scooped black ash from beside the fire into a large shell she'd found earlier on the beach. She added a few drops of water and stirred it with a small stick. The others watched without comment.

Then she crossed to a paperbark tree and carefully peeled some thick sheets off the trunk. 'I don't know how difficult it'll be to write on this but I'll do rough notes for now about stuff that's happened ... starting with us in the tunnel.'

'And hopefully ending with our return trip through the tunnel,' said Jemima.

At the mention of the tunnel Oliver knew his moment had arrived to explain his tesseract-wormhole theory.

'Speaking of the tunnel,' he said hurriedly before anyone shushed him, 'you've heard of wormhole theory, haven't you?' He didn't pause for a response. 'It suggests that time travel *is possible* through short cuts in space-time – what they call cosmic wormholes. They're like tunnels through ...' Meeting Jemima's bemused gaze, he decided to go for a shortened version.

'Well, to get straight to the point, I think that's what's happened to us – the tunnel was a short cut through space-time.' The others were looking at him in mesmerised silence now so he continued. 'Like this.'

He picked up a thin, flexible twig and bent it into a tear shape, so the ends met. 'This is how I was going to explain it the other day, after you came back from Sydney Cove with food – but you didn't ...' He glanced at Jemima. 'Scientists *know* that gravity *can* bend space-time.'

'You're not making any sense, Ollie.' As soon as she said it, Jemima realised she was being mean so quickly added, 'Sorry, go on.'

'Of course it doesn't make sense, Jem. That's why I called it a tesseract tunnel, because a tesseract represents another dimension, something we *can't* understand or imagine.'

'Yeah, but how ...?'

'I don't know how or why, but we could have a problem ...' He was enjoying the limelight so decided to go for a shock element. 'You see, in theory, cosmic wormholes quickly collapse ... which means they're probably only traversable one way ...'

'What? One ...? What are you trying to say?' The others were speaking over the top of each other.

'I'm just saying what the science says.' Oliver realised he'd gone too far.

'I wish you hadn't said *anything* about the tunnel, Ollie. You're freaking me out.'

Oliver bit his lip. He'd read that wormholes *could* stay open to allow two-way travel using quantum effects. *But how do I explain that?* And he couldn't backtrack now.

****

Chapter 32

Reflections

Boorong returned around midday. They were surprised and pleased to see her so soon, but she assured them that she was back and forth across the harbour most days.

'I am free to come and go from Sydney Cove – not like others there,' she reminded them pointedly. In answer to their questions about Ballooderry, she told them she had heard nothing of him yet, but would return to tell them as soon as she had news.

'But I have brought food for you,' she said, sitting among them. 'This tastes good,' she announced confidently, unfurling a roll of soft bark to reveal portions of white meat. She covered them again and placed the bark parcels in the warm coals. The food began to sizzle almost instantly, making their mouths water.

'And this,' she added, placing another bundle in the coals next to the first. 'This cooks fast.' She indicated with her fingers that the pieces were smaller. They nodded gratefully, watching her push the coals around the parcels with a blackened stick. Within minutes she was pulling them away from the heat with her stick and unwrapping the parcels to release steam and a delicious aroma.

'*Pat-tar-rah* – eat it, taste it.' She offered the food around proudly.

Oliver's hand was out first. 'Mm, yum,' he guzzled, with his mouth full. 'Tastes like chicken,' he said, taking another bite.

'Mm,' the others agreed, digging into the juicy chunks.

'What is it?' Jemima said, licking her fingers.

'I don't know the English word,' Boorong replied. 'But that one ...' she pointed to the smaller portions that Archie and Jemima were trying from the other parcel, 'You call that one *grub*.'

'Grub? As in *witchetty grub*?' Jemima asked wide-eyed. She'd just put the bite-size piece into her mouth and bitten into it. 'Actually,' she continued with a wave of her free hand, 'I don't care what it is; it's yummy.'

The others nodded, making appreciative sounds in their throats.

Boorong sat watching them as they finished the meal, with her head to the side and her now-familiar baffled expression. She knew they would be starving without her and Nanberry supplying their food. *Who are they really – these strange young people?* Nanberry had told her they didn't like British food and had only reluctantly eaten it. And they didn't speak like the British or dress like them. They didn't *act* like them.

'You really from here?' She patted the earth beside her. 'You are not from *Yan-nă-dah?*' She pointed to the thin crescent moon visible against the blue sky. She'd made her tone light, trying to make her question sound like a joke. But she looked around at them, waiting for a reaction, as if she thought there was a possibility they were really from another world. She waited for one of them to respond.

'Yes,' Jemima replied eventually, also keeping her voice light. 'We are from here – well, not so far away. But it is different there.'

The others nodded. What could they say? How could they explain their modern lives – their lack of basic survival skills? Boorong nodded too – she would have to be satisfied with that explanation.

After she left, Archie said, 'I've been thinking how crazy it is that we don't know what we can or can't eat here.' He gestured to their surroundings. 'I mean, think about it – without supermarkets, we'd probably starve.'

'At least we have a bit of bush knowledge now, and I'm going to try making a sweet drink from those bottlebrush flowers over there! We soak them in water for a while and the nectar sweetens it – that's what Boorong said.' Millie headed to a bush clustered with crimson blooms.

Oliver, who had stretched himself out on a patch of grass, said,

Reflections

'Well, what I love about here is that I can snooze after lunch.'

****

Several hours later, Millie had moved on from her botanical experiment and was leaning over a thick layer of paperbark spread across a flat rock. It had been surprisingly easy to get her sooty ink into the quill by simply dipping it into the shell – capillary action had filled the hollow shaft of the feather with the black fluid. Then, as she'd drawn the quill tip across the paper, to her delight it had left a mark – though a blotchy one. After persisting, she'd managed to write the first letter of her name clearly, but the other letters had become a mottled patch. However, she wasn't going to give up.

'Okay, I want to ask you all something,' she said, carefully spacing dot points down the paper. 'What's the weirdest or most incredible thing about what's happening to us – as far as you're concerned? Of course, besides the fact we're even here!'

'For me,' said Jemima, 'I think it was going into Mary Mullins's hut and seeing the awful state they live in ... No, actually, it was the amputation.'

'What about the flogging?' Archie spoke up from the other side of the fire. 'That was pretty gruesome – and I couldn't believe how everyone just watched and said nothing ... except the native woman.'

'Yeah, I've thought about that too – how no-one spoke out. I mean, we didn't either, did we?' Seeing Archie about to defend their silence, Jemima put her hand up. 'I know – I know we couldn't do anything about it. But I've been thinking about stuff in *our* time. I mean, there's heaps of bad stuff going on in our time ... and all I've been doing is wearing a t-shirt with *Silence is Complicit* on it and stuff like that.'

'But it's something, I guess,' Archie said, liking this new version of his sister.

'Well, the weirdest thing for me,' said Millie, bringing them back to her question, 'is something I haven't mentioned before because I can hardly believe it actually happened.' She was pleased to see she had their attention. 'When we were at Go-Mo-Ra – the night of the corroboree – I had a visitor at our camp site, after you were both asleep.' She was directing her gaze at Oliver and Jemima. Their eyes widened, but no-one interrupted. 'Yes, um, it was an escaped convict ...'

'What?' her brother and cousins all said at once.

'Her name was Ann Smith and she'd bolted from the settlement just after the First Fleet arrived ... but she was soon lost, and out of food and water, when the local people found her and ...'

'Are you sure this wasn't just a weird dream, cos *you're* freaking me out now.'

'I'm sure. I went swimming with her – in the middle of the night.' The look on Jemima's face said, *This is crazy*, but Millie was beaming. 'It was amazing! And I found this on the beach.' She took the coin from her pocket and handed it to Jemima.

'It's got something written on it but I'd need a magnifier. It's not a coin; it's a medallion or something.' She looked over at her younger cousin. 'But, Millie, what you did was *so* dangerous ...'

'I know – but it didn't seem like it at the time ... There's something else on my mind that I want to ask you all ...' Their eyes were on her again. 'I got an eerie feeling when I first heard Mary Mullins's name – like I had a personal connection – and then, when Boorong mentioned Milbah, I got it again. Do any of you feel like you've been here before? Like ... there's some connection with the people we're meeting?'

'We *have* been here before, Mil,' Archie said with a thoughtful expression. 'We *live* in The Rocks, remember. And of course we have links to the past – it's impossible not to. It's what *déjà vu* means – *already seen* – or something like that? Look, try not to overthink it, Mil.'

'Yeah, I know but ...' Millie's words were cut off by approaching voices, quite a rabble of them. Jemima signalled to keep quiet while she crept to a spot that gave a view over the water to the west. But Archie had already guessed it was the Lump heading back from Parramatta. They sat motionless and silent while it passed Me-Mel, reminded once more of the ever-present danger of being discovered.

****

Chapter 33

Loose Ends

With Archie improving quicker than they'd expected, and the fresh reminder of their vulnerable situation, they began making definite plans for their escape early the next morning. They hoped Nanberry or Boorong would help them.

'I'm going to take a look from that bluff over to Barangaroo Reserve,' Jemima announced. 'See if I can get any clues to where the entrance to the cave is – it has to be there.'

Oliver and Millie jumped up to join her.

From the elevated position they had a good view of the area that would become modern-day Millers Point and the western side of the ridge where Windmill Street ran down the hill towards Barangaroo Reserve.

'Wow, things are sure going to change!' Jemima said as she gazed across the water in the direction of the dense forest covering the slope. She tried to work out where the Hero of Waterloo hotel would be built. In modern Sydney it was hidden from the waterfront by a jumble of concrete and steel. She was trying to remember roughly when it was built when a frightening fact occurred to her.

'It's not built yet!' she blurted, meeting her cousins' startled looks. 'The Hero – it doesn't even exist yet – it wasn't built till the 1800s, so the tunnel can't be there either.' Jemima shook her head slowly. 'So how do we get back if there's no tunnel there yet?' She glared at Oliver as she posed the question. 'Come on, Mr Know-All, answer that. How do we get back?'

Oliver opened and closed his mouth, but Millie jumped in.

'Look, don't even let your mind go there, Jem. Our first step is to find the cave. We have to believe the tunnel's behind it and will lead us home. So let's just concentrate on step one.'

Jemima made no reply, embarrassed by her outburst. She shaded her eyes and scanned the rugged landscape and then down along the water's edge.

As Millie cast her eyes over the same area, she realised she was fingering the metal disc in her pocket and, just for a second, she wished it could be a lucky charm that led them home.

'Look,' said Jemima, breaking into Millie's thoughts. 'There's the beach we found when we first arrived.'

The other two nodded and continued combing the escarpment for other natural features that might be familiar.

With one eye closed, Millie ran her extended finger up the slope from the beach. Then, with a sudden intake of breath, she said, 'See that area with golden wattles in bloom, among those massive boulders, and a cliff face behind? I think that's where the cave entrance is. See, there's a really rugged section below it that runs down to join those rocks where we saw all the oysters.' She did a little happy dance. 'The tunnel's where the wattles are – I remember smelling them when we came out of the cave. I'm sure that's it! High five!'

Oliver slapped his palm against hers with a grin.

'Good work, Mil, but how do we get there from here – we'd be too exposed to just head towards that beach in broad daylight.' Jemima continued searching the hillside with intense scrutiny. 'And then we have to make our way uphill, and it's steep. We have to be sure where we're going this time.'

'That scary man we met – he was giving us directions – we just didn't realise it at the time. If we start from where we met him – which was further around the headland into Darling Harbour, what Boorong calls Go-Mo-Ra – and past the rocks covered with oyster shells, from there he said we should head up and across the ridge – I think that's to where there are lots of she-oaks growing together – and then head back at an angle. It's almost like a triangle. So if we trace an angle from the oyster-covered rocks to, say, halfway up the slope and then at a forty-five degree angle back again, it takes us to that grove of wattles growing within those huge boulders. It has to be it!'

'Good work again, Mil. Okay, let's head back and work out a plan with Archie. We also have to discuss what we're going to tell Nanberry and Boorong.' Jemima didn't wait for a response. 'They assume we're heading over the mountains, so I think we should leave it at that. I don't think we should mention the tunnel – it'd be far too complicated to try to explain.'

Millie agreed wholeheartedly. Oliver didn't mention he'd already asked Nanberry about tunnels or caves in the area. *He's probably forgotten anyway*, thought Oliver.

Back at the camp they went over what they'd seen with Archie, stressing that it would be a tough climb from the beach up to the cave entrance, especially without shoes.

'I'm getting used to having bare feet now,' Oliver announced. 'It feels good, especially on the sand.'

'Well I, for one, like wearing shoes,' Jemima retorted. 'What happened to yours, anyway, Ollie? You still had them when we left you sitting under the rock shelf.'

'Good question. I either left them there, or dropped them when I was racing downhill, trying to keep up with Nanberry. It's a bit of a blur.'

'Anyway, if Boorong or Nanberry come back later, hopefully they'll say they can help us get over there early enough in the morning not to be seen.'

****

Boorong returned late afternoon with the news that her brother, Ballooderry, had wounded a convict as payback for the destruction of his canoe and that, as a consequence, the gov'nor had banned him from coming into the Sydney settlement *and* the Parramatta settlement. She was fuming.

'He may be shot on sight if he puts his foot into Sydney Cove,' she told them. 'The gov'nor said my brother is an *outlaw* now – because he took the law into his own hands. But the British don't understand our ways. We have our own laws.' Boorong was wringing her hands in anger and frustration.

'My brother's spirit is broken ... he trusted the gov'nor. He is hiding now and my people will not let him be taken to the British prison. Nanberry will warn him if the soldiers are on their way.'

Jemima put her hand out to comfort Boorong, but she moved away.

'*Min-yin?*' Boorong said over and over, shaking her head in distress, before looking directly at each of them. 'Why? I am asking *why* the gov'nor decided this. Before, he offered good things to my people, but now, what is happening it is *weree* – it is *bad*.'

'Yes, it is – I am so sorry for the things that are happening to your people, Boorong.'

'Yes,' said Boorong, in a softer manner. 'I am sorry too – they think their way is better. The gov'nor made promises to Bennelong, and so my people went to live in Sydney Cove. But the gov'nor does not always listen to them now.'

'Yes. It's a bad situation, Boorong. And we think we should leave tomorrow morning, before – well, before it gets worse. Will you help us?'

'Yes, I will help you. And Nanberry will help you. You must leave early – before sunrise. Do you know your way now?'

They told her about the scary man they'd met and how he had given them directions – though they were careful not to spell out exactly what he'd said.

'That is Pemulwuy,' she said immediately. 'He thinks we do not need more strangers here.' She smiled to herself. 'So he is happy to show you the way to leave. He does not believe the promises of the gov'nor as Bennelong and others still do. He believes our ways are better and he will fight to keep our ways strong.' She looked at them with an expression that said, *and now I agree with him*.

Then, changing the subject, Boorong said, 'Mary also wants to leave here. She told me again today. She said she will meet you – and go with you.' When no-one responded, she said. 'Mary said she helped you and you must help her. She said she wants to see a better life ...'

'We need to discuss this, Boorong – it's a huge decision.'

'But it is Mary's decision. I told her I would bring her to meet you – when you leave. I will tell her you will leave tomorrow morning and we will meet her.' It was clear this was Boorong's way of saying they owed Mary Mullins. 'She said her ma won't need her now she's got Mr Peat.'

'But, Boorong, you don't understand ...'

'Now that you know your way, she can travel here the same way you did, if that place does not suit her.' Boorong nodded as if to say *and that is final*. 'We will come here before sunrise and take you to Parramatta – we must leave very early to avoid the Lump.'

'Parramatta?' They looked at Boorong in confusion, and she stared back in equal bewilderment.

'Yes. You are going over the mountains?' She looked from one to the other, and they looked at each other awkwardly. 'It will be easier if you begin your journey – your walking – from Parramatta ...'

Seeing her logic, Jemima jumped in with a reply. 'Thank you, Boorong – you have done so much to help us, but it is better if we return the way that's familiar to us – the way we came. And that's from the western slope over there.' She then turned slightly and pointed in the Barangaroo Reserve direction.

'It is a long way to walk from there to the mountains – but as you wish. I will ask Mary to be at the point before sunrise – the place where Archie hid. It is easy to bring the nawis close to shore there. Then we will take you to our Go-Mo-Ra camp. And that is where we will say goodbye.' She gave a twisted smile, looking at each of them. Then, glancing towards the paperbark sheets spread over the flat rock, she said, 'Who is writing a journal?' She walked over for a closer look and Millie followed her.

'Me.' Millie looked down at her illegible words surrounded by blotchy ink marks and then back at Boorong. 'I want to write about what's happened to us here, and about you and Nanberry ... but it doesn't look so good.' She began laughing and Boorong joined her.

'I can read some English, but I cannot read that,' Boorong said, still giggling. 'It is good to laugh, Millie.' She looked more closely at the writing and pointed to a word. 'I can see my name there. But, Millie, why do you want to write about me?'

'Because I want people where I live to know about you and what has happened here – to you – and your people.'

'And will you write about what happened to Ballooderry?' Boorong had become serious again.

'Yes, I will, Boorong – I think people where I live *should* know all about what happened to your brother. And also the way Mrs Johnson cared for you and Mr White cared for Nanberry. And about your meetings with Mr Dawes at Tar-Ra, and about the laughter and friendships you made together there ... and how things can be better ... when people listen to each other ... when people are kinder ...'

Millie had a lump in her throat by the time she finished, and when she looked around she saw that everyone had gone quiet. It was as if they had all become aware how significant this experience had been and that it was coming to an end.

'Yes,' said Boorong as she rose to leave. 'It is good to learn new ways, but Pemulwuy says it is important not to forget the old ones.' She nodded her head in farewell. 'I will return tomorrow morning.'

****

Chapter 34

The Scramble

They were waiting on the beach when Boorong and Nanberry slid their nawis onto the sand at Me-Mel. It was barely light but a chorus of kookaburras was already heralding sunrise with their raucous chortling.

'Thank you so much for helping us ... again,' Jemima said as their friends helped Archie into one of the vessels.

Nanberry and Boorong's plan was still to meet with Mary and, in silence, they propelled their nawis towards a small crescent of sand at the end of the point at Tar-Ra.

They were about halfway across the harbour when the movement of soldiers, near their destination, caught their attention. Their red jackets stood out against the foliage in the pale early morning light.

Several of them noticed the nawis heading across the water and waved. Nanberry and Boorong immediately changed direction, veering towards Darling Harbour – past the rocky outcrop where oysters clung to the rock platforms and out of sight. Once they had rounded the headland they all heaved a sigh of relief.

'I think it was still too dark against the water for them to see who was in the nawis – I think they'd only see outlines. But this is not good for Mary – she was meant to wait there for us. When she sees we can't land there ... I don't know ... maybe she will go to the rock overhang where she first met you all, and wait there.'

They continued paddling past the little beach that Jemima had planned their course from, and were heading to the Go-Mo-Ra camp site. *Our route will need a rethink now*, Jemima thought.

Boorong spoke to Nanberry in their language, but repeated it in English. 'Who do you think the soldiers are looking for?'

The Scramble

'I don't know. Maybe they are looking for more clues about the escape, or maybe they found signs of someone hiding there.' He looked at Archie. 'Or maybe someone told them Mary was planning to leave and they were sent to stop her.'

'But she's not a convict – surely she has the right to leave,' Millie's voice held disbelief.

'But after the Bryant escape, more convicts will be getting ideas about ... *doing a bolt*, they call it. The gov'nor said as much, and they are restricting anyone with a boat now. So, anyone with ideas of escape will be looking to the west rather than the sea. There are already stories about your land of plenty over the mountains.'

'Yeah, they wouldn't want it to start a trend,' Jemima said under her breath. 'And women are in short supply too, I s'pose.'

'Oh yes,' said Boorong catching her words. 'That is one reason Mary wants to leave. She said she already has smelly convict men eyeing her.' Then Boorong's voice took on a worried edge. 'I hope they are not looking for Ballooderry. I hope he hasn't been foolish enough to come into the settlement. I know he already sent word to Bennelong to ask if the gov'nor is still angry with him. And the gov'nor sent a message to say, *Yes – he is still angry.*'

They were pulling into the landing spot at Go-Mo-Ra, and Nanberry was about to reply, when a series of gunfire rang through the air. They cringed in fright.

'Sounds like it's coming from Tar-Ra, but it could be closer. Quickly, you must go. I hope you find Mary ... and your way home.'

Boorong was clearly tense now as they scrambled out of the nawis and headed for the cover of the forest. The urgency of the moment allowed no time for drawn-out goodbyes.

'I bid you well,' Nanberry called after them simply, and they turned fleetingly to wave.

They only paused once they had reached the deep shadows of the forest, where Jemima took control.

'This way, guys.' She was leading the way up to their right.

'No, Jem. Isn't it this way?' Millie pointed up and across to their left. 'Remember, we worked out that we need to keep the rocky outcrop to our left and that will eventually take us up close to our first camp – under the rock overhang. And this is the way Boorong came out of the forest when she came over the ridge to visit us at Go-Mo-Ra. Remember?'

The others were gazing up the slope in uncertainty when Jemima said, 'You're right. I'm getting confused. Okay – let's go.'

'Wait, we need to agree on the route first.' Millie said. 'Once we reach – or can at least see – our first camp site, that's the marker to turn downhill at about a forty-five degree angle ...'

'Why do we need to go up and then back again? Why can't we cut directly across the slope?' Archie queried, eyeing the steep, rugged slope ahead of him. He was already feeling drained of energy.

'Because there's a ridge or spine that cuts across and down the slope, and we'd be forced to backtrack. It seems like a short cut that way, but it's not.' Millie spoke with confidence. 'That's what Pemulwuy was trying to explain to us but we were so scared we weren't taking it in.'

Archie smiled at Millie's uncharacteristic assertiveness and gestured as if to say, *Lead the way.*

'So we need to head more north –'

Gunfire, sounding closer, cut off Oliver's comment and spurred them up the hillside. All talking ceased while they struggled up the rugged incline, picking their way between trees and bushes, and around rocks, repeatedly losing their footing on the steep sections.

Archie looked pale when they stopped to catch their breath but he insisted he was okay to carry on.

Finally, further up the slope, they saw the site where they'd spent their first night in Sydney Cove. They scanned the area from a distance, searching for Mary waiting for them. But the place was deserted.

'We have to wait for her,' Millie said with a tremor. 'We can't just leave ... we can't.'

'She had about the same distance as us to cover, though from a different direction. So, if we managed to get here, she should be here by now, if she's coming.'

'She could've changed her mind. And I hope she has.'

'Shouldn't one of us take a closer look?'

'It's way too dangerous to wait another second. We should keep going. There could be soldiers closing in on us, for all we know. Come on. Going downhill should be easier but, I have to say, my legs feel like jelly.'

They'd been heading downhill at a hectic pace for what seemed like a very long time, when Archie tripped and fell for the third time. When the others scrambled back to help him, they were looking up the slope and saw they'd overshot the place they were looking for. Oliver pointed to the stand of golden wattles among huge boulders, and the others simply nodded – they were too exhausted to speak. Retracing their steps, then changing course towards the rocks, they finally reached the small clearing in front of the cliff face, and dropped to the ground in the exact spot they had been days earlier.

'Okay, this is it, isn't it?' Jemima said, breathless from exertion and nervous energy. 'This is the right spot, and it's the moment of truth. This tunnel is either taking us home, or it isn't.'

In that instant, gunfire resounded again through the forest, followed by a shout – *or was it a scream?* It wasn't far away. No-one said a word – there was no need. They scrambled frantically across the loose stones and around the edge of the massive rock that hid the entrance to the cave. And they were gone, soon enveloped in the darkness that they hoped would lead them back past tree roots dangling into the cavity, past the initials carved in the sandstone wall, and to the light at the top of the rough-cut stone stairway.

****

Tunnel to Tar-Ra

... and another world

Epilogue

Sydney Daily News Online

Time will tell

A young woman, who wishes to remain anonymous, has approached a Sydney museum with an artefact believed to have great historical significance. The item, described by its owner as a copper coin, was found on a Sydney beach over two hundred years ago by her convict ancestor who arrived on the First Fleet. 'At least, that's how the story goes,' she said.

Historians declared the 47 mm copper disc to be a 'priceless item' as it is engraved on both sides with details of the First Fleet's voyage. It dates to 1788, making it one of the first European artworks made in Australia. Its creator is believed to be convict, Thomas Barrett, who also produced a silver medallion under orders from the fleet's surgeon John White. Now known as the Charlotte Medal, the silver piece was purchased for three quarters of a million dollars in 2008 and is displayed at the National Maritime Museum, Darling Harbour.

The young woman, also an emerging author, said her medallion recently resurfaced in a tin beneath the floorboards of their family home in The Rocks. Its discovery prompted her to continue working on stories set in Australia's colonial times. When asked why she thinks history matters, she said:

'I remember the poem by Oodgeroo Noonuccal:

'Let no one say the past is dead.

The past is all about us and within.'

'So, we can't ignore the past,' she said emphatically. 'My brother, who's studying physics, says the latest science also suggests that past and present are inseparable. It's all to do with space-time, which is pretty awesome! However we look at it, the past matters. Check out the 'Centre for Time' on Sydney Uni's website.'

Time present and time past
Are both perhaps present in time future
And time future contained in the past.

Extract from T. S. Eliot's poem 'Burnt Norton'
(No. 1 of 'Four Quartets')

References

Bowes Smyth, Arthur, 'The Journal of Arthur Bowes Smyth: Surgeon, Lady Penrhyn 1787 - 1789'. Published by, Sydney, Australian Documents Library Pty Ltd, 1979, (original copy made 1789-1790).

Clark, Ralph, 'The Journal and Letters of Lt. Ralph Clark, 1787 - 1792', published by, Sydney, Australian Documents Library Pty Ltd, 1981.

Collins, David, 'An account of the English Colony in New South Wales, Volume 1 (of 2), Illustrated edition', The Echo Library, 2008, (originally published 1798).

Dawes, William, 'Dawes Notebooks on the Aboriginal Language of Sydney, 1790-1791', Hans Rausing, 'Endangered Language Project & School of Oriental and African Studies', London, 2009. See: https://www.williamdawes.org

Fowell, Newton, 'The Sirius Letters: The complete letters of Newton Fowell 1786 - 1790', Published by The Fairfax Library, 1988, Nance Irvine, editor.

Hunter, John, 'An Historical Journal of Events at Sydney and at Sea 1787 – 1792', published by Angus & Robertson, Sydney 1968. Search for the online version at the Project Gutenberg.

Hunter, John, 'An Historical Journal of the Transactions at Port Jackson and Norfolk Island'. https://www.gutenberg.org/ebooks/15662

Johnson, Reverend Richard, 'Letters from the Rev. Richard Johnson to Henry Fricker, 30 May 1787-10 August 1797'. https://acms.sl.nsw.gov.au/_transcript/2010/D01866/a1769.pdf

King, Lt. Philip Gidley, The Journal of Philip Gidley King: Lieutenant, R.N. 1787 - 1790, published by, Sydney, Australian Documents Library Pty Ltd, 1980.

Old Bailey Proceedings Online: https://oldbaileyonline.org/index.jsp

Pain, Daniel, 'The Journal of Daniel Paine 1794-1797', published by the Library of Australian History, Sydney, 1983 edition, (in association with the National Maritime Museum Greenwich, England).

Tench, Watkin, '1788', 'Comprising, 'Book One: A Narrative of the Expedition to Botany Bay, 1789' and 'Book Two: A complete Account of the Settlement at Port Jackson'. Introduced and edited by Tim Flannery, Text Publishing, Melbourne, 1996.

Worgan, George, 'Journal of a First Fleet Surgeon', the William Dixon Foundation, Library Council of New South Wales, Sydney, 1978.

White, John, 'Journal of a Voyage to New South Wales, 1790', published by J. Debrett, London.
See the online version at Project Gutenberg.
https://gutenberg.net.au/ebooks03/0301531h.html

Historical Notes

Note: Journal authors, for example Watkin Tench, refer to 'transactions' in their chapter titles which means 'events'.

Chapters 1- 3
There are no historical notes for chapters 1 to 3.
Refer to the map, on page vi of modern Sydney showing Windmill Street and Barangaroo Reserve etc.
Information about the cellar and tunnel beneath the Hero of Waterloo hotel go to: 'Our famous cellar & tunnel' at: https://heroofwaterloo.com.au/history/

Chapter 4 - Where on Earth
No historical notes for chapter 4.
See page vii for the map and images of Sydney Cove in 1790s, showing Tara and the Sydney Cove settlement buildings: hospital, barracks, Governor's House, etc.

Chapter 5 - Reality Dawns
Details of convicts chained while working or wearing large iron collar 'with two spikes projecting from it' see:
Tench, '1788', 'Book Two: A Complete Account of the Settlement at Port Jackson', Chapter 13, 'The transactions of the colony continued to the end of May, 1791', P. 184.

Details of friendly meetings at Tar-Ra (Dawes Point) between Lieutenant William Dawes and a number of Eora see:
Dawes, William, 'Notebooks on the Aboriginal Language of Sydney, 1790-1791'.
Rausing, Hans, 'Endangered Language Project & School of Oriental and African Studies', London, 2009.
For Dawes and Rausing, see: https://www.williamdawes.org/

Chapter 6 - Adjustment

Nanberry's account of the British coming ashore is based on several accounts by First Fleet journalists, see:

King, Philip, Gidley, 'The Journal of Philip Gidley King: Lieutenant, RN. 1787 -1790', notes for January 18th 1788.

Worgan, George, 'Journal of a First Fleet Surgeon', Library of Australian History, p. 6.

Worgan describes the Eora confusion about the gender of the white men and the questions they posed to the British.

For an account of the first hanging in the Sydney settlement (convict Thomas Barrett) see:

Collins, 'An Account of the English Colony in New South Wales, Volume 1 (of 2)', Chapter 1, February 1788.

Clark, Ralph, 'The Journal and Letters of Lt. Ralph Clark', p. 102, February, 1788.

White, John, 'Journal of a Voyage to New South Wales'; 27th February.

Bowes Smyth, Arthur, 'The Journal of Arthur Bowes Smyth: Surgeon, Lady Penrhyn 1787 - 1789', Feb, 1788, p. 75.

Chapter 7 - Nanberry

Nanberry as an 'interpreter':

Tench, '1788', 'Book Two: A Complete Account of the Settlement at Port Jackson', Chapter 8, 'Transactions of the Colony in the Beginning of September, 1790.'

For an account of Nanberry's first contact with the British and his early days in Sydney Cove, see:

Tench, '1788', 'Book Two: A Complete Account of the Settlement at Port Jackson', Chapter 4, 'Transactions of the Colony in April - May, 1789'.

For an image of Nanberry in his blue jacket, see Natural History Museum collection, Drawing no. 3 of the Watling Collection:

'Nanberry, a native boy of Port Jackson' (Painting attributed to George Raper).
https://nhmimages.com/search/?searchQuery=Nanberry

Details on the atrocious condition of convicts who arrived on the Second Fleet, see:
Collins, 'An Account of the English Colony in New South Wales, Volume 1 (of 2)', Chapter 10, detailing the arrival of the Second Fleet' June 1790.

Chapter 8 - The Find
For an account of Arabanoo's contact and experiences with the British, see:
Tench, '1788', 'Book Two: A Complete Account of the Settlement at Port Jackson', Chapter 3, 'Transactions of the Colony, from the Commencement of the Year 1789, until the End of March'.

Note: Watkin Tench was present at Arabanoo's first dinner at Government House, but in his final published journal he didn't mention Arabanoo's belief that the British intended eating him. We know of the incident through a private letter from Lt. Newton Fowell to his father in 1790, see:
Fowell, N., (originally 1790), 'The Sirius Letters: The complete letters of Newton Fowell 1786 - 1790', Sydney: The Fairfax Library, (Nance Irvine, editor, 1988)

For Nanberry's early days in Sydney Cove and his adoption by John White, see:
Tench, '1788', 'Book Two: A Complete Account of the Settlement at Port Jackson', Chapter 4, 'Transactions of the Colony in April and May 1789'.
For account of smallpox among the Eora, see: Collins, 'An Account of the English Colony in New South Wales, Volume 1 (of 2)', Chapter 7 (April – May 1789). Also see Appendix VIII, Diseases.

Chapter 9 - Night Sounds
No historical notes.

Chapter 10 - Strangers
Ann Harmsworth, Mary Mullins and Henry Kable 'junior' were among fifty children who sailed with their parents aboard the First Fleet, landing in Sydney Cove in January 1788. See their details in Chapman, Don, '1788: The People of the First Fleet Sydney', Doubleday Australia Pty Ltd, 1986.

Convict, Henry Kable senior was appointed as a constable and night watchman, as well as later receiving a free pardon, see:
'Australian Dictionary of Biography' online: www.adb.anu.edu.au

From 1791, rumours circulated among convicts that a place of plenty existed beyond the Blue Mountains where 'copper-coloured people would treat them kindly.' Some believed China was only a few days walk from Sydney to the north (or south), west or across a river. In late 1791 there were a number of attempted escapes, see:
Tench, '1788', 'Book Two: A Complete Account of the Settlement at Port Jackson', Chapter 15, 'Transactions of the Colony to the end of November, 1791'.
Hunter, John, 'An Historical Journal of the Transactions at Port Jackson and Norfolk Island', Chapter 23.
Collins, 'An Account of the English Colony in New South Wales, Volume 1 (of 2)', Chapter 15, November 1791.

Chapter 11- Separation
Natives were fired at for 'stealing' potatoes near Tar-Ra.
Collins, David, 'An Account Of The English Colony in NSW, Volume 1 (of 2)', Chapter 12, January 1791.
Mention of amputations in early Sydney, see:
Tench, '1788', 'Book Two: A Complete Account of the Settlement at Port Jackson', Chapter 17, 'Miscellaneous Remarks on the Country'.

Collins, 'An Account of the English Colony in New South Wales, Volume 1 (of 2)', Chapter 28, gives details of the leg amputation of a soldier, Nicholas Downie.

Chapter 12 - Mary Mullins

An El Niño event occurred in the early 1790s causing severe drought in eastern Australia, see:

Grove, Richard H., 'The Great El Niño of 1789–93 and its Global Consequences' in 'The Medieval History Journal, 10, 1&2 (2007)', p. 75–98, Sage Publications.

Tench, '1788', 'Book Two: A Complete Account of the Settlement at Port Jackson', Chapter 17, 'Miscellaneous Remarks on the Country'. This account gives details of the weather for the summer of 1790.

For details about Mary Mullins and her mother, Hannah Mullins' crime and transportation, see:

Chapman, Don, '1788: The People of the First Fleet, Sydney'. Doubleday Australia Pty Ltd, 1986.

Chapter 13 - Mr Peat

See Charles Peat's court record in the 'Old Bailey' records, 5 Dec 1781 for highway robbery on horseback; 'assault and robbery' of coach passengers.

Also, for his escape, 7 July 1784, known as 'returning from transportation' for further background see:

http://www.fellowshipfirstfleeters.org.au/charlespeathanna hmullens.htm

Chapter 14 - The Flogging

For details of Eora present in Sydney Cove at a convict's flogging for stealing an Aboriginal women's fishing tackle, see:

Tench, '1788', 'Book Two: A Complete Account of the Settlement at Port Jackson', Chapter 13, 'Transactions of the colony to the end of May 1791'. This account gives details of Barangaroo (Bennelong's wife) finding a stick and attacking the flogger, and Daringa sobbing.

Chapter 15 - Oliver
No historical notes.
Tesseract:
https://www.scienceabc.com/pure-sciences/what-exactly-is-a-tesseract-real-life-geometry-4-dimensional.html
Bending of space-time:
https://www.esa.int/esearch?q=space+time+curvature
https://bigthink.com/hard-science/a-controversial-theory-claims-present-past-and-future-exist-at-the-same-time/

Chapter 16 - Boorong and Patye
Boorong was found dying on a beach and brought to the hospital at Sydney Cove in April 1789 suffering from smallpox. She was estimated to be at least 13 years-old at the time. After recovering she lived with the Reverend Richard Johnson and his wife Mary for at least 18 months, see:
Tench, '1788', 'Book Two: A Complete Account of the Settlement at Port Jackson', Chapter 4, 'Transactions of the Colony in April and May, 1789'.

For reference to Dawes' close friendship with Aboriginal people and in particular with a young woman Patyegarang, see:
Dawes, William, 'Notebooks on the Aboriginal Language of Sydney, 1790-1791'.
Rausing, Hans, 'Endangered Language Project & School of Oriental and African Studies, London, 2009'.
After mastering English, Boorong and Nanberry routinely 'interpreted on both sides' for the Eora and British. For a Nanberry example, see:

Tench, '1788', 'Book Two: A Complete Account of the Settlement at Port Jackson', Chapter 8, 'Transactions of the Colony in the Beginning of September, 1790', page 134.

Chapter 17 - The Stash
No historical notes.

Chapter 18 - Dilemma
For a description of the Eora use of clay body paint and decoration, see:
Collins, 'An Account of the English Colony in New South Wales', Volume 1, Appendix II - Stature and Appearance.

For William Bryant's role as the colony's chief fisherman, see:
Collins, 'An Account of the English Colony in New South Wales', Volume 1, Chapter VI.

Chapter 19 - Go-Mo-Ra Camp
See map on page vi showing Go-Mo-Ra (Darling Harbour)
Regarding Eora women fishing with a fire alight in their nawis for cooking their catch, and singing while fishing see:
Collins, 'An Account of the English Colony in New South Wales', Volume 1 (of 2), Appendix IV-Mode of Living.

Details of their 'pelican song' see:
Dawes, 'The Notebooks of William Dawes on the Aboriginal Language of Sydney', Book C, p. 15.

Boorong's name meaning 'star', see:
Collins, 'An Account of the English Colony in New South Wales, Volume 1 (of 2)', Appendix XII—Language, sub-title, 'Names chiefly of objects of sense'. Collins uses the spelling Bir-rong for star; Hunter uses Birrang for the stars; Daniel Paine's journal uses Borong for star.

Boorong is cited as having a unique knowledge of the stars, see: Collins, 'An Account of the English Colony in New South Wales, Volume 1 (of 2)', Appendix VII-Superstition.

Chapter 20 - Night Visit
Ann Smith's court proceedings and sentencing in August 1786 at the Old Bailey see: www.oldbaileyonline.org/

Regarding Ann Smith's escape on 14th February 1788, see:
Bowes Smyth, Arthur, 'The Journal of Arthur Bowes Smyth: Surgeon, Lady Penrhyn 1787 - 1789', p. 72. 'This day Ann Smith (the woman who refused taking the slops on board from Mr. Miller the Commissary) eloped from the camp, as she often, when on board, declared she would as soon as she was landed'.

Chapter 21 - Sky and Water
Dingo is an Eora word for Australia's native dog and Tench was the first to record the word 'dingo', see:
Tench, '1788', 'Book One: A narrative of the Expedition to Botany Bay', Chapter 11.
Recorded as din-go in Collins' journal, 'An Account of the English Colony in NSW'; Appendix XII-Language.

Chapter 22 - Archie
Convict John Wilson, was described by David Collins (Sydney Cove's Judge Advocate), as 'a wild idle young man, who, his term oftransportation being expired, preferred living among the natives in the vicinity of the river, to earning the wages of honest industry ...', see: Collins, 'An Account of the English Colony in New South Wales, Volume 1 (of 2)', Chapter XXVIII.

Ballooderry was the nineteen-year-old brother of Boorong, from the Burramattagal clan of Parramatta, who in 1791 'lived chiefly at Governor Phillip's house'. Hunter's spelling is Ballederry, see:

Hunter, 'An Historical Journal of the Transactions at Port Jackson and Norfolk Island', Chapter XXI, 'Transactions at Port Jackson, April 1791 to May 1791'.

Chapter 23 - Voices
In March 1791 there was a corroboree at Bennelong's Point and for an account and detailed description of song and dance 1791, see:
Hunter, 'An Historical Journal of the Transactions at Port Jackson and Norfolk Island', 'Chapter VIII, February 1791 to March 1791'.

Chapter 24 - Learning Curve
For the translation of 'boojery caribberie' as 'good dance' along with the edible grasslike plant that Boorong refers to is Lomandra Longifoli and commonly known as basket grass, see:
Hunter 'An Historical Journal of the Transactions at Port Jackson and Norfolk Island'; 'Chapter VIII, February 1791 to March 1791'.

Chapter 25 - Millie
For the varied Eora meanings for 'white', see:
Tench, '1788', 'Book Two: A Complete Account of the Settlement at Port Jackson', Chapter XVII, 'Miscellaneous Remarks ...' p. 249.
Quote: 'It may be remarked, that they translate the epithet white, when they speak of us, not by the name which they assign to this white earth [white ochre]; but by that with which they distinguish the palms of their hands.'

Chapter 26 - Choices
John Hunter sailed from Sydney Cove late March 1791, see:
Collins, 'An Account of the English Colony in New South Wales, Volume 1 (of 2)', Chapter XII, sub-heading 'March'.
Details of the punitive expedition that William Dawes was forced to join, see:

Tench, '1788', 'Book Two: A Complete Account of the Settlement at Port Jackson', Chapter 12, 'Transactions of the Colony in Part of December, 1790'.

Nanberry did fulfill his plans to become a Gadigal warrior and a sailor on British ships: He was one of fifteen Aboriginal youths initiated at a ceremony called Yoo-long Erah-ba-diahng or 'operation of drawing the tooth' in February 1795, see:
Collins, 'An Account of the English Colony in New South Wales, Volume 1 (of 2)', Appendix VI-Customs and Manners.

Nanberry sailed on various British ships from the 1790s. Explorer Matthew Flinders mentions Nanberry sailing with him aboard HMS Investigator in 1802, see:
Flinders, Matthew, edited and introduced by Tim Flannery, 'Terra Australis', Text Publishing, 2012 ('A voyage to Terra Australis' was first published in 1814).

For reference to 'The Lump', a barge used to transport provisions to and from Sydney Cove and Parramatta. The 'launch' as referred to by Collins was originally called, by convicts, the 'Rose Hill Packet' and later referred to 'The Lump', see:
Collins, 'An Account of the English Colony in New South Wales, Volume 1 (of 2)', Chapter VIII, October 1789.

Also see: https://gutenberg.net.au/ebooks/e00010.html (CTRL F to find 'Lump'.

Chapter 27- Dead End
Descriptions of Eora men's body adornments see:
Collins, 'An Account of the English Colony in New South Wales, Volume 1', Appendix II, 'Stature and Appearance'.

Worgan, George B., 'Sydney Cove Journal: 20 January - 11 July 1788', (Penned in 1788, it was reproduced by the Banks Society publications with introduction & notes by J. Currey, 2010).

Pemulwuy's English skills are confirmed, see:
Collins, 'An Account of the English Colony in New South Wales, Volume 2 (of 2), Chapter IV, (ie, his conversation with officers and Collin's spelling is Pemulwy)

Chapter 28 - Tar-Ra
Account of what happened to Ballooderry's nawi and the consequences see:
Collins, 'An Account of the English Colony in New South Wales', Volume 1 (of 2)', Chapter XIII
Tench, '1788', 'Book Two: A Complete Account of the Settlement at Port Jackson', Chapter 15, 'Transactions of the colony to the end of November 1791', p. 203-204.

Eora view of justice: 'seeks fair and open combat only', see:
Tench, '1788', 'Book Two: A Complete Account of the Settlement at Port Jackson', Chapter 17, 'Miscellaneous Remarks on the Country', p. 262.

Chapter 29 - Night Walkers
For the escape of William and Mary Bryant see:
Tench, '1788', 'Book Two: A Complete Account of the Settlement at Port Jackson', Chapter 13, 'The Transactions of the Colony continued to the end of May', subheading 'March' 1791', p. 180.

Collins, 'An Account of the English Colony in New South Wales, Volume 1 (of 2)', Chapter XII, sub-heading, 'March'.

Chapter 30 - Me-Mel
The island of Me-Mel in Sydney Harbour is also known as Goat Island. For details of Bennelong's connection to Me-Mel see:

Collins, 'An Account of the English Colony in New South Wales, Volume 1 (of 2)', Appendix IX, Property. Here Collins refers to Me-Mel as Bennelong's property or real estate.

Chapter 31- Revelations
No historical notes.
See wormhole theory:
https://www.britannica.com/science/wormhole
https://www.space.com/20881-wormholes.html
www.scientificamerican.com/article/wormhole-tunnels-in-spacetime-may-be-possible-new-research-suggests/

Chapter 32 - Reflections
Eora diet (honey, yams, fern-root, various flowers) see:
Collins, 'An Account of the English Colony in New South Wales, Volume 1 (of 2)', Appendix IV, Mode of Living.

For coins produced by convict Thomas Barratt, on the First Fleet voyage see:
White, 'Journal of a Voyage to New South Wales', 5th August 1787.

For the 'Charlotte' medal and copper version made by Thomas Barrett in 1788, see:
https://www.sea.museum/search?query=charlotte+medal

Chapter 33 – Loose Ends
For the disagreement and ensuing issues between Ballooderry (Hunter's spelling is Ballederry) and Governor Phillip, see:

Hunter, 'An Historical Journal of the Transactions at Port Jackson and Norfolk Island', Chapter XXII, Transactions at Port Jackson, June 1791 to September 1791.
Collins, 'An Account of the English Colony in New South Wales, Volume 1 (of 2)', Chapter XIII, June 1791.

Chapter 34 - The Scramble
No historical notes.

Epilogue
For scientific notions of time, see:
https://bigthink.com/hard-science/a-controversial-theory-claims-present-past-and-future-exist-at-the-same-time/

Also, see 'The Centre for Time', University of Sydney.

Character Information

Fictional characters

Archie
Jemima's brother. Oliver and Millie are his cousins.

Jemima
Archie's sister. Oliver and Millie are her cousins.
She is the eldest of the four time travellers.

Millie (Milbah)
Oliver's sister. Archie and Jemima are her cousins.

Oliver
Millie's brother. Archie and Jemima are his cousins.

Characters as recorded in the journals, letters, diaries and reports of the British in early Sydney Cove years. (1788 – 1792)

Aboriginal people

Arabanoo
Arabanoo was the first Aboriginal man to be captured on Governor Phillip's orders. Although he was initially terrified at being taken to the Sydney settlement he, over time, became friends with Governor Phillip, many of the marines and convicts.

Balloderry
Balloderry was an Aboriginal youth of the Burramattagal clan and he was Boorong's brother. He was a good friend of Governor Phillip. However this friendship changed for the worst when Balloderry, seeking retribution his for his nawi (canoe) was being smashed, speared an innocent convict at Parramatta.

Barangaroo

Barangaroo was Bennelong's wife and a member of the Cammeragal clan. Barangaroo and Bennelong had been known to have a passionately volatile relationship moving between heated arguments to showing tenderness and devotion to each other. Barangaroo died, in 1791 not long after the birth of their daughter Dilboong.

Bennelong

Bennelong was a member of the Wangal clan. He was the second indigenous man, along with Colbee, to be captured. Although Bennelong and Colbee eventually escaped they did come in contact with the British again. Bennelong became good friends with Gov. Phillip and with many of the British in the Sydney Cove settlement.
On Phillip's return to England in 1792, Bennelong agreed to go with the governor. Bennelong arrived back in Sydney Cove in 1795.

Boorong

Boorong was a member of the Burramattagal clan. She was an indigenous girl who survived the small pox in Sydney Cove. After recovering from the smallpox, in 1789, she was taken into care by the Rev. Richard Johnson and Mary Johnson. Boorong went on to be an interpreter between her people and the British.

Nanberry

Nanberry, was an Aboriginal boy of the Gadigal clan. He, like Boorong, survived the smallpox in Sydney Cove. He was taken into care by the surgeon, John White. Nanberry learnt enough English to be an interpreter between his people and the British.

Patye (Patyegarang)

Patyegarang was a young Aboriginal woman believed to be of the Cammeragal clan. Patye, after a number of visits to William Dawes's observatory at Tar-Ra became close friend with Dawes. She played a very important part in assisting Dawes compile his notebooks which became a major source of information about the Aboriginal people's language of Sydney.

Pemulwuy

Refer to the Historical Notes for Chapter 27 – Dead End. In this chapter where time travellers meet an Indigenous warrior, Susan implies that the warrior is Pemulwuy. In chapter 33 Boorong confirms it was Pemulwuy. He was of the Bidjigal clan and was a fierce resistance fighter who opposed the British incursion.

Convicts living in Sydney Cove in 1791

William and Mary Bryant

William and Mary were from the same fishing district in England. They were married in February, 1788. William was entrusted with the oversight of the colony's fishing operations. His and Mary's situation changed when he was found guilty of selling fish privately. After receiving lashes and being moved from his hut he earnestly commenced meticulous plans for an escape. In late March 1791, the Bryants with their two young children and seven convicts, on a moonless night set sail for Batavia. In just over two months they landed at Kupang, Timor, where they were eventually discovered to be escapees and transported to Batavia, Indonesia.

Anne Harmsworth (convict's daughter)

Anne was the daughter of Private Thomas and Alice Harmsworth. Thomas died of illness in April 1788. Her mother, Alice, in October 1971 married Daniel Stanfield and they settled on Norfolk Island. In January 1800 Anne married Samuel Marsden, a shoemaker.

Kable - Henry, Susannah and Henry Jnr.

Henry and Susannah met in Norwich prison in England and it was where Henry Jnr. was born. They couple were married, in the new settlement, in February, 1788. Henry and Susannah were successful in the colony by creating a profitable shipping and mercantile business. Henry Kable Jnr went on to be a sailor and a master of sailing ships.

Mary Mullins (convict's daughter)
Mary was born in 1785, the daughter of Edward and Hannah Mullins. She accompanied her mother to Sydney Cove on the First Fleet ship the *Lady Pehrhyn*. It has been noted that no record of her life or subsequent death in the new colony has been found.

Mr Peat
Charles Peat (aka Charles Peal) was tried at the Old Bailey 1785 and sentenced to transportation for life. In February 1788 he and Ann Mullins were married. He worked as an overseer of timber-getters, was appointed to the night watch later gaining the status of night watch principal. Peat received a conditional pardon in 1795.

Ann Smith
Ann was a nurse aged twenty-nine when she was convicted for stealing. During her voyage on the *Lady Penrhyn* and upon arrival in Sydney Cove she said she would escape. She absconded on the 14th of February, 1788. There is no conclusive evidence as to her fate.

John Wilson
Wilson was found guilty of a felony in 1785 and sentenced for transportation on the First Fleet. It is suggested that David Collins referred to Wilson as 'a wild young man …' when his term expired Wilson lived with Aborigines for several years.

Officials and marine officers living in Sydney Cove in 1791

David Collins (Colonel)
Collins was a British Marine officer who was appointed as Judge – Advocate to the new colony. As well as fulfilling his judicial tasks, Collins also wrote a detailed two volume journal covering many aspects concerning life and conditions in the early years at Sydney Cove.

William Dawes (Second Lieutenant)
Dawes was an astronomer and engineer. He had an observatory built, at Tar-Ra, with a cone shaped whitewashed canvas roof with a special flap that opened to view the stars. Although Dawes was a surveyor and explorer he is perhaps best remembered for notebooks detailing the language of the Sydney Aboriginal people.

Reverend Richard and Mary Johnson
Richard Johnson came to the colony as Chaplain to the First Fleet and for some time was the only clergyman in New South Wales. Boorong was adopted by the Johnsons after her smallpox recovery. At the request of Boorong, the Johnson's first born daughter was given an Indigenous name of Milbah.

Governor Arthur Phillip
Phillip was the commander of the First Fleet, eleven ships that sailed on the thirteenth of May, 1787, from, Portsmouth, England. He was made Governor of NSW in October, 1786. It has been noted that, 'by 1788 Phillip was fifty years old and had developed a cool, controlled disposition balanced with fair-mindedness; he was a humane man but he could mete out hash justice when necessary'.

Watkin Tench (Lieutenant General)
Tench is the author of two accounts, 'Narrative of the Expedition to Botany Bay' and 'Complete Account of the Settlement at Port Jackson' which provide an account of the arrival and first four years of the colony. Tench was on friendly terms with several of the Aboriginal people who regularly visited the Sydney settlement.

John White (Chief Surgeon)
White was in charge of the colony's hospital and worked hard to treat the sick and injured. White was in the first exploratory expedition west of the colony in April, 1788. He was a keen botanist. After Nanberry's smallpox recovery, he was taken in by White.

Acknowledgements

As Susan Boyer's husband I extend the first acknowledgment to my late wife. Susan has always been an inspiration to me and more so from witnessing the time she put into writing 'Tunnel to Tar-Ra' and research for a PhD through Western Sydney University (WSU). In the latter stages of her being with us she continued writing to complete her manuscript. Being with and seeing Susan's storytelling passion and diligence, while contending with health issues, was something special to experience.

Susan's PhD supervisors at WSU, Doctor Dianne Dickenson, Professor Susanne Gannon and Adjunct Associate Professor Carol Liston, are to be commended. Their dedication to supporting Susan during her research work and the writing of 'Tunnel to Tar-Ra' was exceptional.

Uncle Gregg Simms, Gadigal Elder at WSU, assisted Susan in relation to The Rocks, Gadigal country precinct of Sydney. For Uncle Gregg's time and knowledge sharing, Susan was very thankful.

Dharug cultural consultant, Christopher Tobin, has collaborated with Susan on other projects. Again, Chris gave his time with care and respect. Thank you for providing valuable manuscript appraisal and advice on cultural aspects relating to Indigenous content in 'Tunnel to Tar-Ra'. Your assistance was invaluable and highly appreciated by Susan.

I am indebted, on both Susan's and my behalf to Distinguished Professor Larissa Behrendt and Professor Susanne Gannon for making the time to read and provide editorial comments and give positive feedback on Susan's manuscript. The uplift for Susan from Larissa's and Susanne's involvement, at a critical time of manuscript completion, cannot be understated.

Dr Catherine Heath AE took on the copyeditor process for 'Tunnel to Tar-Ra'. I am very grateful for her involvement as Catherine went beyond the 'call of duty' to provide corrections as well as story enhancements to Susan's manuscript. There is absolutely no doubt that Catherine's detailed editing provided a solid keystone to Susan's novel.

Thank you Jennie Vanderjagt for your insightful feedback and thoughts on Tunnel to Tar-Ra's future teacher and classroom use.

A book needs a cover and much gratitude is extended to Julie McVey for creating the cover artwork and to Matt Thompson for completing the cover graphics design.

Susan's son, Clinton Bagley and I took on a role that Susan would have dearly loved to finish. That is, we fine-tuned the story flow and yet still have it remain true to her original words. I was continually amazed by Clinton's eye for detail to make many suggestions that I hope will make 'Tunnel to Tar-Ra' a thrilling and enjoyable story to read.

Leonard Boyer (Publisher) June 2024

Images and Quotes

Page v map: Adaption of a map created in 1822.
Source: National Library of Australia - nla.obj-229911701-1

Page vi map: Modern Sydney shoreline – 2020's
Sourced from Maps Data: Google©2024

Page vii map: A View of Sydney Cove, Port Jackson, 7th March 1792
Source: Natural History Museum (London)

The use of Oodgeroo Noonuccal's words in the Epilogue from her poem 'The Past' was granted by publishers Wiley.
This permission was approved via CCC Marketplace.

The use of T.S.Eliot's words from his poem 'Four Quartets' was granted by Faber Permissions.

Publisher's Note

The characters, Oliver, Jemima, Archie, and Millie appearing in this story are fictitious. Any resemblance to real persons, living or dead is purely coincidental.
Other characters in 'Tunnel to Tar-Ra' were recorded as living in or near the British settlement in Sydney Cove, during the years of 1791 and 1792. The events of the flogging, corroboree and the Bryant's escape, as witnessed or heard about by the four teenagers are from recorded historical documents, such as, journals, letters, diaries and reports.

About Susan Boyer

Towards the middle of 2021 Susan started experiencing some body discomfort. Medical tests in mid-August 2021 revealed a diagnosis of pancreatic cancer. At this stage she still had four chapters of 'Tunnel to Tar-Ra' to finalise, as well as write the references and historical notes.

It was because of Susan's, determination, passion and courage that saw her manuscript completed. Even up to a couple of weeks before her passing, in February 2022, she worked on story feedback changes and the historical notes. 'Tunnel to Tar-Ra' was also a component of her work towards a PhD through Western Sydney University. In late 2022, due to the quality of Susan's writing and research, she was awarded a posthumous Doctorate of Philosophy.

Susan's writing career started in the late 1990's. While teaching English language and literacy at TAFE NSW she saw the lack of Australian English learning material. In 1998 she published her first book 'Understating everyday Australian – Book One' with an accompanying audio. This book and audio is still in demand in the 2020's. Susan went on to author 25 titles and produced 10 accompanying audio resources.

In 2013, Susan transitioned from a teaching career into becoming a full-time researcher, writer and presenter with a focus on early Australian colonial history. Since 2014, she presented author talks in schools, libraries and to historical groups. She gave radio interviews and published articles on the importance of true, inspirational stories from Australia's past. And her own words, perhaps, best describes her historical writing passion, 'My wish is that, like me, those stories will leave you wanting to know more'.

Susan has left an incredible legacy as an author, researcher, presenter and educator.

For more information on Susan see: www.susanboyer.com.au

Across Great Divides:
true stories of life at Sydney Cove

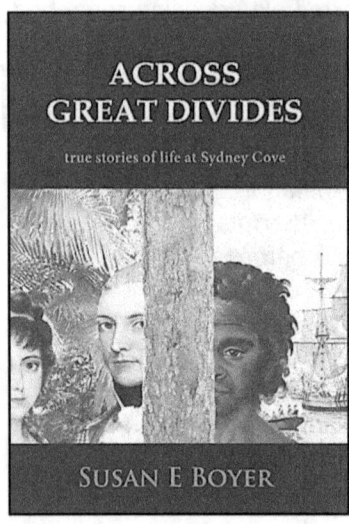

'All communication with family and friends now cut off, we are leaving the world behind us, to enter a state unknown'.

So wrote David Collins aboard one of eleven ships entering the vast unchartered waters of the Southern Ocean in 1787.

'Across Great Divides - true stories of life at Sydney Cove', brings to life the diverse experiences of people living in the precarious circumstance of Australia's first penal colony. The stories are relayed through a non-fiction narrative.

All the stories relate to the people and actual events as recorded in journals, letters and official reports of the First Fleet.

The stories also give voice to the dilemma of the Aboriginal people challenged by the unexpected arrival of white people to their land.

Read the different perspectives of military men volunteering for a tour of duty in the remote colony.

The book contains bibliography, index and detailed notes on original sources.

Australian history - Non-fiction - RRP $26.95
ISBN 9781877074424

Available from all major online booksellers

Australian curriculum links and free teacher resources @ www.birrongbooks.com

'Stories of Life at Sydney Cove', follows the success of 'Across Great Divides'. It is written for younger readers as historical fiction, but the stories are about real people.

* * * *

When thirteen-year-old convicts, John and Elizabeth, are sent to a mysterious land at the end of the world, they have no idea what life holds for them. At Sydney Cove there are no roads, no fences, or buildings... just wilderness. Later when Indigenous children Nanberry and Boorong come to live with the white strangers, they see life through different eyes.

'Stories of Life at Sydney Cove'
Susan E Boyer
ISBN: 978 1 877074 49 3
Available from online booksellers

Find free teaching and learning resources at www.birrongbooks.com
See links to Australian History and English Curriculum below:
Version 8.4, (Yrs 3-6) and Ver 9.0 (Yrs 7-10)

Year 4 - Learning area content descriptions
Stories of the First Fleet, including reasons for the journey, who travelled to Australia, and their experiences following arrival. (ACHASSK085)
The nature of contact between Aboriginal and Torres Strait Islander Peoples. (ACHASSK086)
Year 5 - Learning area content descriptions
The nature of convict or colonial presence, including the factors that influenced patterns of development, aspects of the daily life of the inhabitants and how the environment changed. (ACHASSK107)
The role that a significant individual or group played in shaping a colony. (ACHASSK110)
Year 9 - Making and transforming the Australian nation (1750–1914)
The causes and effects of European contact and extension of settlement, including their impact on the First Nations Peoples of Australia. (AC9HH9K03)